THE CORNER OFFICE

Ashutosh Garg worked in the corporate sector for over twenty-five years before starting Guardian Pharmacy, a nationwide chain of health and wellness retail outlets, in 2003. Today, Garg sits on the board of several NGOs and companies, and has also written the highly acclaimed book *The Buck Stops Here: My Journey from a Manager to an Entrepreneur*.

THE CORNER OFFICE

ASHUTOSH GARG

RUPA

Published by
Rupa Publications India Pvt. Ltd 2013
7/16, Ansari Road, Daryaganj
New Delhi 110002

Sales centres:
Allahabad Bengaluru Chennai
Hyderabad Jaipur Kathmandu
Kolkata Mumbai

ISBN: 978-81-291-2477-7

10 9 8 7 6 5 4 3 2 1

Printed at Repro Knowledgecast Limited, Thane

To my wife
Vera
and
my sons
Varun and Ashwin

I have met hundreds of corporate managers
on their deathbeds over the years.
Not one of them, in their dying wish to me, has said,
'I wish I had run a bigger company.'
'I wish I had made more money.'
'I wish I had more power.'
All of them, unanimously, have said,
'I wish I had been a better husband.'
'I wish I had been a better father.'
'I wish I had been a better human being.'

—An eighty-year-old Jewish rabbi, speaking at an international conference

Contents

Prologue

It was the year 1980. The new decade had started with a leap year.

The world population had just crossed 4.4 billion.

John Lennon had been assassinated, Idi Amin had been overthrown, the Rubik's cube was taking the world by storm and the video game Pac-Man had become a rage. Jimmy Carter was the president of the United States of America and Margaret Thatcher the first woman prime minister of the United Kingdom. CNN was launched as the first international news channel.

Changes were taking place in India as well. The dark days of the Emergency were over and there was optimism in the air. Yet, there was a whole generation of young people who had faced the Emergency as students, and felt insecure and uncertain of what their government would do for them.

The Mandal Commission had been set up the previous year to identify the socially or educationally backward. This would lead to severe discontent and disagreement in later years.

Zulfikar Ali Bhutto had been executed in Pakistan the previous year and tensions between the two countries had been considerably exacerbated. Sri Lanka defeated India in the 1979 Cricket World Cup. The Indian hockey team won the gold medal in the Olympics and provided a much-needed boost to the youth of the country.

Rishi Kapoor was the new heart-throb of the young nation. The films *Qurbani* and *Karz* were setting new standards for Bollywood. Sangeeta Bijlani had been crowned Miss India and the Indian cricket team was beginning to make its presence felt on the international stage.

The seventh Lok Sabha elections were held and in spite of all the uncertainties, the Congress alliance won 374 seats. Indira Gandhi was back in power after three years in the wilderness and Sanjay Gandhi was killed in a plane crash.

India was looking forward to a period of stability and growth after the uncertain leadership of Morarji Desai and Charan Singh. Economic growth had reached 5.5 per cent, a number that would be classified later by economists as the Hindu rate of growth, and would provide a benchmark for future finance ministers of the country. However, in socialist India, for the bureaucrats and politicians, profit was still a dirty word.

The Indian Administrative Service was the aspiration of every bright young college graduate, followed by admission into the Indian Institutes of Technology, only to look for jobs in USA once their course had been completed. At the same time business schools in India had started coming into vogue during the mid-seventies, and parents were beginning to understand that there was a life beyond being a doctor, lawyer, engineer or an IAS officer. A master's degree in business administration was now seen as a passport to a great career in the growing corporate sector.

A new generation of young starry-eyed managers was graduating from these business schools and other educational institutions. Goaded on by their parents, these young men and women were eagerly looking forward to leaving their mark on the world.

Trust Corporation

Trust Corporation had been set up in India at the turn of the twentieth century as a subsidiary of a major American liquor-manufacturing corporation. Seeing the size of the Indian population in then British-ruled India, the American managers of Trust Corporation, USA, had decided that selling alcohol in the country would be an attractive business proposition. They launched a very low-end alcohol to test the market.

'Distributing free alcohol samples would be a great way to enter this market,' one of the young managers had concluded in a presentation to his seniors, based on the simple premise that anything free was always appreciated and once the consumers had gotten used to the heady brew, they would keep coming back for more.

'Give the natives a type of alcohol they have never consumed before,' he had told his colleagues.

Over the last seven and a half decades, Trust Corporation had grown into a major powerhouse in India. The company was also seen as an excellent employer and was keenly sought by youngsters looking for a career in the corporate world.

The organization had never stopped any of its managers from consuming alcohol after office hours. However, it had a clear rule that if any manager had had a drink, they would not drive. In such a case, every manager was allowed to either hire a car with a driver and be dropped home, or take a hotel room and stay the night, at company expense.

For Trust Corporation, protecting its reputation by preventing the event of an accident under influence of alcohol was far more important than the expense incurred to do so.

Over the years alcohol had generated large cash flows for the company, which had to be put to good use by investing in other businesses. So, after selling alcohol in India for over seventy years, it had diversified into software and power. The alcohol business was churning out more than 100 per cent of the profits every year, more surplus cash than Trust Corporation could handle. But the management had recognized the stigma attached to selling alcohol; therefore the decision to expand its portfolio.

While power was capital intensive and socially relevant, software was the new emerging opportunity in the eighties that could earn a lot of foreign exchange for the country. Trust Corporation, like so many other Indian business groups, had thus decided to embark upon this exciting business venture.

The company, often referred to as a 'cradle to grave' organization, was well known for its policy of hiring young managers and grooming them in its culture, providing them training in various businesses and giving them excellent career opportunities. All the board managers, directors and even the chairman of the company had started their careers with Trust Corporation as management trainees and worked their way up. None of them had ever felt the need to work for any other.

Jobs in Trust Corporation were much sought after in business schools, as well as in the professional community, such as chartered accountants and lawyers.

'Every soldier carries a baton in his knapsack' is the army's way of saying that every soldier can aspire to become a field marshal. Trust Corporation believed in this line in letter and spirit, and managers in human resources had always endeavoured to provide an environment where every manager could aspire to become the chairman of the group.

Located on the second floor of the company building was the office where the chairman operated from. Popularly referred to as 'The Corner Office' within the company, the chairman sat in a 2,500-square-foot office with its own reception area, a separate seating area for two secretaries, a boardroom for meetings with senior members of management, a private bathroom and shower, and a separate elevator. As one entered the corner office, one could sense the power that went with the position.

The chairman's table was a fifty-year-old Burma teakwood desk, and every chairman had retained the same table, since it had history embedded in every particle. Each leg of the table had a stylized carved 'T', which was the company logo. It had no drawers and no partitions. This was to allow complete transparency in spirit and fact about the individual and the corporation. On the side table were three black telephones, one an intercom through the secretary, the second a direct telephone line and the third a hotline to the international headquarters on Long Island, New York.

The room had white marble flooring and wood-panelled walls polished a natural brown. There were three separate sofa sets, and the centre table for each sofa set was placed on an expensive carpet.

Occupying this office was what every young manager who joined Trust Corporation aspired for. Over the course of their careers, these managers would play games with one another, plot, collude and do whatever possible to get ahead of their peer group in the race leading to the corner office.

~

1980

Five young managers had been offered the position of management trainees in various disciplines in Trust Corporation. Selection to this category was done only once in every five years. Since the management was looking for future leaders and board members, taking in a batch every year would have led to unnecessary and unhealthy competition.

These five came from varied family backgrounds with different qualifications. Children of middle-class families, all of them had been born in the early or mid-1950s, a generation of 'post-Independence' children. They were the 'baby boomers' of India. The late seventies and the early eighties presented heady career and growth opportunities for the educated and fired by ambition, they were all determined to change their country and the world.

Emerging from the shackles of colonialism, with politicians waxing eloquent about Gandhian philosophy and Nehruvian idealism, they had been given an excellent education by their ambitious parents, who wanted to see their children make a mark for themselves in this young nation. They had grown up in an environment where their parents had, at every opportunity, reminded them of the sacrifices made by the political classes to gain Independence. 'We fought the British to get you independence' was the standard line the children of the fifties heard, leaving a lot of them feeling highly indebted.

Over three hundred young men and women had applied for the five management trainee positions in Trust Corporation. Applications had come from top business schools in India and overseas, top engineering colleges across India, qualified chartered accountants, undergraduates and lawyers. Sifting through this mass of applications was a slow and arduous task that was taken very seriously by the human resources department. The selection process started in December of the given year and was generally over by March of the following year, in time for completion of the academic sessions in most colleges.

The applicants had been through gruelling group discussions and several rounds of interviews before their selection, and they knew that once they were selected, they were 'set' for the rest of their lives. The management training programme of the company, often referred to informally as the Trust School of Business, had been designed on the lines of the prestigious Indian Administrative Service to develop future leaders for the organization.

The interviewers had quizzed them on matters ranging from specialization of their education, current affairs, world economy, sports, girlfriends or boyfriends and family backgrounds. The final round had taken them to the hallowed portals of the corporate offices, where they were invited to dine with the board members.

The selected few were flown to New Delhi for their final round of meetings with the board of directors. Like most young people of their age, they had not had an opportunity to board a plane before this, so each of them selected a hopping flight rather than a direct one, thereby giving themselves an opportunity to land and take off more than once and get two sets of meals.

Arrangements had been made for them to be picked up

from the New Delhi airport. As each of them pulled their bags off the luggage carousels and wheeled their trolleys out of the airport, they were met by a liveried chauffeur and driven to the company guest house in a fancy car. This was a lavish guest house offering every comfort, usually reserved for the top management. A young executive from the human resources department met each of them and showed them to their rooms.

'Welcome to Delhi and to Trust Corporation,' the executive said. 'I have the responsibility of looking after you while you are here.'

By dinner time, all of them had arrived. Rahul Jain, Raj Dhingra, Sangeeta Malhotra, Iqbal Mohammad and Anita Fernandes sat together in the drawing room, looking at and sizing up one another.

'Hi, I am Rahul from Shimla,' he began, taking the lead in the introductions. 'I am an engineer from IIT and have an MBA with a marketing major from IIM Ahmedabad. I am looking forward to getting to know you better.'

Sangeeta, who was standing next to Rahul said, 'I am Sangeeta Malhotra. I am also from IIT and have done my MBA from Harvard. While I am delighted to be with all of you, I must say that my first choice would have been to work in USA, had it not been for the recession in that stupid country.'

Iqbal took the cue next. 'My name is Iqbal Mohammad. I am from Lucknow. I am a chartered accountant and unlike all of you, I have been hired for the finance function. Trust Corporation is very serious about finance and I am sure that one day I will run this company.'

Not wanting to be left behind, Raj said in his faltering English, 'Myself Raj Dhingra and from Chandigarh, Punjab. I am educated in Hansraj College, Delhi, and did MBA from

Chandigarh. We will be getting to know each other and I am sure I will be having a lot of fun in our training.'

All four of them looked at the last candidate, a small-built dusky girl with large eyes. She had above average looks and a voluptuous body.

She looked nervously at her future colleagues and said, 'I am Anita. I am lucky to be here today because of the blessings of our Lord Jesus Christ. I have specialized in human resources, so I guess I won't really be competing with all of you.'

They knew that they would be colleagues and friends for several years. But as they sat together in this first meeting, they had not even begun to imagine the intense competition and rivalry they would face with one another, as their respective careers progressed over the years.

All of them knew that they would compete for the ultimate job of chairman of Trust Corporation. They also recognized that there could only be one person who would make it to the position. Yet, at their current starry-eyed stage, none of them was willing to even consider the idea that the winner could be anyone other than himself/herself. For the moment, as they sat together, they thought of the opportunities they had been provided and, like most middle-class Indians who had been taught to fear and thank God, muttered a silent prayer of gratitude to the Almighty.

After politely declining the drinks that the guest-house bearer offered them, they had dinner at the large dining table. No one really had an appetite, thinking of the meetings the following day, but all of them nibbled at the food on the table, made polite conversation and then decided to turn in early.

They had been told that they would be picked up from the guest house the following morning at 10 a.m. to visit the corporate office for their meetings with senior management and lunch with the board of directors.

An air-conditioned Matador van, not a very common sight in 1980, was standing outside the guest house to take them to the corporate office the next morning. All five of them had had their bed tea in their rooms and were ready early. They smiled nervously at one another at the breakfast table.

Each one was formally dressed, the men in dark suits and white shirts with red, green or blue ties and the women in pastel-coloured sarees and matching blouses with their hair tied back, giving them stern and serious looks. Unsure of what to expect, faint beads of sweat could be seen on all their foreheads.

~

The corporate office of Trust Corporation, located on a large ten-acre campus in the heart of New Delhi, was an imposing four-storey building built over fifty years ago, with tall Victorian columns. Driving through the long tree-lined boulevards, they reached the imposing head office building, which was painted sparkling white, with black windows and doors accentuating the whiteness of the building.

Although the building was located on a busy road where the traffic did not seem to come to a halt, once inside there was relative peace and tranquility. Thick walls and double glazed windows muted all external sounds. There was an atmosphere of relaxed urgency and quiet efficiency as one looked around the area outside the building.

The car park was clearly marked, with the senior managers being allocated parking slots closer to the entrance of the building so that their walk to the office would be shorter than the rest. The names of the directors on the board with their car numbers below were painted on small wooden plaques affixed to the walls of the car park. Efficient security regulated the movement of the pedestrians and vehicles within the campus. As the five trainees walked past, each of them imagined a day when their own brand-new vehicles would be stationed next to plaques with their names and car numbers.

The white marble lobby with the imposing marble staircase and shining brass railings, along with the old but efficient lifts with collapsible brass gates, were indicators of the heritage and age of the corporate office. Maintenance of all this brass was a full-time task for three people.

The reception desk was made of white marble with a highly-polished Burmese teakwood top. The logo of Trust Corporation had been carved on the front of the desk. Rumour had it that this desk was as old as the company and had been used by the first chairman before it was replaced by the larger and more imposing one that now occupied centre stage in the chairman's office.

Behind the reception desk sat Mrs D'Souza, a stern-looking middle-aged Anglo-Indian lady with half-moon spectacles perched on the tip of her nose. She was always aware of who came in and went out of the building. She had been the receptionist for as long as anyone could remember. Over the years Mrs D, as she was commonly referred to, had developed the ability to read the faces of managers after a meeting. She could tell who had a good meeting with the board and who did not. Anxious managers in various locations of the company would call her to check if the presentations made by their bosses had been completed and what her impressions were of that meeting.

'How was the presentation, Mrs D?' someone would ask her over the phone.

'Your boss looked very worried,' she would reply. 'I don't think the proposals were accepted by the board.' She would enjoy hearing the groan of disappointment from the other end.

Mrs D'Souza also knew about all the secret affairs of the younger male and female managers, about habitual latecomers and those who left office early. She was a treasure trove of personal information. Nothing was hidden from her and she revelled in the little power this information gave her.

The senior peon sat next to her on a wooden stool, dressed in a well-starched white uniform with the Trust Corporation logo on the lapels. He had earned this position after many years of loyal service. Only the best-performing senior peons were entitled to sit next to the receptionist as the face of the company. This was the second most powerful position amongst the peons, the top one being the peon posted to the chairman's office, who would be seated outside the corner office.

Mrs D'Souza greeted the five young management trainees at her reception desk with a simple handshake and said, 'Welcome to Trust Corporation. I wish you lots of happiness and success in your lives and careers.' She had said the same thing to dozens of other trainees over the years.

Rahul shook hands with her warmly and said, 'Good morning, Mrs D'Souza.' He had taken the trouble to ascertain her name from the guest-house attendant.

Sangeeta and Anita smiled and said hello.

Iqbal nodded his head to acknowledge her presence but did not shake her hand. He did not like shaking hands with ladies.

Raj did not even bother to look at her. For him, she was only a receptionist.

Why are all of them wishing a receptionist so warmly is beyond my apprehension, he thought.

Mrs D'Souza noticed all of them and memorized the reaction of each one. She would reciprocate in an appropriate manner when she got an opportunity. She had never been one to forget anything, especially when she felt insulted.

She called the peon and said, '*Baba log ko upar boardroom me leke jao.* (Take the children to the boardroom.)'

In the boardroom, the human resources (HR) department had arranged a series of presentations, giving information about the company and its senior managers. The five were asked to take a seat around the huge rectangular table.

Colourful and professionally-made flip charts, brochures and leaflets were used to explain the various businesses of Trust Corporation. The trainees were told that each of them would be assigned to a division of the company or the function they had been specifically selected for in the first few years and, based on their performance, they would be moved across divisions and roles. Growth in the company, they were told, was entirely based on meritocracy. The top management believed in letting the 'best candidate win'. After the presentations were done, each of them asked a few polite questions that they had prepared in advance, so as to be noticed by the presenters.

At exactly 1 p.m., they were taken to the lunchroom and introduced to the board members. All five of them were star-struck. Here were managers whom, so far, they had only read about in business magazines and newspapers. The trainees introduced themselves politely and confidently to the smiling group, who, looking at them, remembered their own nervous steps several years ago when they had joined the company.

Once the introductions were over, the five youngsters looked on in amazement at the sheer opulence of the wood-panelled lunchroom.

'Please have a seat,' the vice-chairman of the company said to them as he took his place at the head of the table.

The lunch table in the directors' dining room was laid out with a lavish multiple-course meal. Liveried waiters stood silently, unobtrusive yet attentive, waiting for the slightest wave of a hand or imperceptible nod to serve the next course. The staff had been advised in advance about the meal preferences of each person, and consequently several types of dishes were available. However, given their nervousness and the occasion, none of the five dared to refuse anything served. They had been taught that the easiest way to handle so much cutlery and crockery was to start with whatever was outermost and work inwards. That way, one could not go wrong.

Grape shears with matted vine-leaf handles were kept next to the grape bowl. If any of them did decide to eat some, they were expected to use the grape shears to cut a bunch of grapes, use the shears again to pick it up and dip the grapes in a glass of water to clean them before eating.

They were observed closely by members of the board as they ate their lunch. They had been trained properly and could see the nods of approval from the board members from the corner of their eyes.

Towards the end of lunch, the chairman walked in and was introduced to them. He had obviously done his homework and knew each of them by their first name. He shook hands warmly, welcoming them to a long and successful career in Trust Corporation.

They knew they were the chosen few.

They had been selected into the covenanted cadre of the company management. The company often compared its management training programme to the pre-Independence

Indian Civil Services and believed that its managers were capable of handling any business at any location in the country.

What the five had not realized was the burden of the roles each was expected to play and the expectations that the corporation would place on each one. They would soon learn of the all-pervasive role the company would play in their lives and how they would not have time for anybody else, any other activity, as long as they worked for Trust Corporation.

Trust Corporation would not only take over their work lives, but also their social lives and that of their spouses.

~

The management training programme was designed to put them through their paces. It was extremely intense and every trainee was expected to work round the clock for the entire one-year period. Top management and senior managers were expected to take time out of their busy schedules to train them in a classroom as well as on-site. The five were also taken to visit all the facilities of the company, spread across the length and breadth of India.

The HR department was responsible for mentoring these five young trainees during the first year. In addition to the training schedule that was to be followed very carefully, HR was also mandated to observe each individual—their likes and dislikes, their threshold for work pressure, their interpersonal skills and what business of the company did they take a strong liking to. A similar report was also taken from every senior manager who met these trainees.

The one year they spent as management trainees passed very quickly. During this time, they travelled across the country, learning the businesses and spending time with various company managers and personnel. They realized that every person could not be treated the same way. Each one's identity was defined first by his caste, then his state and finally as an Indian.

They learned to identify the powerful managers within the company. They learned that the company management had strong camps, and sooner or later they would be expected to align themselves to one camp or the other. They tried to understand who to align with and who to stay away from.

They related with managers who they sensed were supportive of the learning process and they learned to be cautious of those who were dismissive of the entire management training programme. They met secure managers who were moving ahead quickly in the company and insecure ones who were not growing as fast as they had expected to, and were therefore very cynical.

Most importantly, they started to understand one another.

They started to see each one's strengths and weaknesses, and realized that when it came to the crunch, it would really be each on his or her own. Every one of them was very ambitious. Some expressed their ambition openly, while others nursed it quietly. But the fierce determination with which they went through the training programme gave the HR managers reason to believe that once again, the company had selected the next set of leaders with the care and concern that was expected of them. The HR director would keep a close eye on the performance of these five as they were groomed for leadership roles.

'Let the best person win' was the company philosophy.

Soon, the time had come for these managers to be sent out into the operating divisions and functions of the company and prove their mettle.

All five of them needed to start their climb up the steep and opportunistic 'corporate ladder'.

Rahul

Rahul Jain was born in 1956, into a middle-class family in Shimla, Himachal Pradesh. His father was a mid-level Government of India officer who would often tell him, 'Beta, on my small salary, all that your mother and I can give you is an excellent education and very strong values, which hopefully will stand you in good stead all your life. I cannot leave any wealth for you other than this small house.'

What else do I need? wondered Rahul.

He had always been taught the values of honesty and the need to hold his head high.

His mother was a well-educated, God-fearing woman who never had the courage to oppose her husband. She was content with running the house and staying in the background.

'*Bhagwan se darna, jhoot mat bolna aur chori mat karna* (fear God, tell the truth and don't steal)' was the regular message ingrained into him day after day by his mother.

Rahul got his values, ambition and drive from his father. Though only a mid-level government employee, his father always pushed Rahul to excel in everything at school and college.

'You must achieve everything that I was not able to,' he would tell his son.

Rahul learned to thank God for everything he achieved in

his life. Thirty years later, he still carried the Hanuman Chalisa he had got from his mother in his briefcase wherever he went. Every time he was faced with a crisis or any kind of uncertainty, he recited the forty verses of the Hanuman Chalisa to put his mind at peace.

Jai Hanuman Gyan Gun Sagar
Jai Kapis Tihu Lok Ujagar
Ram Doot Atulit Bal Dhama
Anjani Putra Pavan Sut Nama

His childhood was happy, but like most middle-class teenagers of his age in a newly emerging nation, there was nothing of consequence that he could remember from that period. He always had a full stomach, he played in the gardens outside his home in the evenings and he improvised with what he had to occupy himself. An old wooden clothes beater, when discarded by his mother, became a handy cricket bat. Bricks were used to set up wickets and old tennis balls discarded by the local club were sufficient to get the local kids to start playing cricket.

Rahul, an exceptionally gifted child, was always in the first or second position in class. He was also very competitive and rebuked himself if he did not top his class.

As he reached class ten, his parents started talking about college, though they were able to provide him little guidance.

'He knows what he has to do. I have full faith in him,' his father would tell his mother every time she chided him for not worrying about their son's career.

Rahul never had too much pocket money throughout school and he always remembered how difficult it was for his mother to make ends meet on the small salary his father earned. Unlike a lot of his friends' parents, who seemed to have an unlimited supply, his father was an honest government employee and had never believed in taking a bribe.

Rahul remembered how his mother would increase his trousers' length as he grew taller since her budget did not permit her to buy new trousers for him. He also recalled how she would turn his short collars inside out when the right side of the collar frayed because of excessive wear and washing.

His idea of fashion was to stitch a red triangular patch on his old trousers so that they were shaped into 'bell-bottoms', which was the rage in those days. His prized possessions were two silk shirts, made from old silk sarees that had been handed down to his mother by a wealthy aunt.

Like so many of his peers, he too applied for the entrance examination of the Indian Institute of Technology and was selected for an engineering degree from one of the top colleges in India. Later, he could remember very little of his IIT days. As he reached his final year, he realized that he needed to study further. He had the choice of either staying in India or going to USA, like so many of his batchmates were planning to. He chose to stay back and decided that in order to get an edge, he had to obtain a degree in business administration. He decided to take the Common Admission Test for the Indian Institutes of Management and was selected to IIM Ahmedabad.

Rahul majored in marketing and on completion of his two-year MBA programme, he was selected as a management trainee in Trust Corporation.

~

Working in the corporate world with Trust Corporation created a powerful identity for everyone, and it was no different for Rahul.

His mother started receiving marriage proposals for the

eligible young bachelor, but Rahul was convinced that there was no way he could spend his life with a girl he had been introduced to over a cup of tea. He had often debated the merits of arranged marriage with his mother and had come to the conclusion that while this system worked in India, he was not willing to go along with it, but would choose his own soulmate.

'Ma, I understand you want me to get married, but you know I cannot possibly spend my life with someone whom I have not gotten to know better,' he would always tell his mother.

'But your father and I had an arranged marriage and see how happy we are,' his mother would reply.

'Times have changed, Ma. Girls are much more independent and they will not always accept what the husband says, as you have done all your life with Papa,' he would respond. 'Give me time and I know I will find the right person for myself.'

As a young management trainee, he was assigned to the marketing function of the alcohol division, from which the company made all its money. The first year involved a lot of travel with the company salesmen, visiting remote markets to understand the powerful distribution system. Senior managers of Trust Corporation believed that they could get any product to the remotest part of the country within twenty-four hours. Working in the markets was a huge learning experience for Rahul.

The company permitted two club memberships for all its managers. Like the other four management trainees, Rahul also got corporate memberships to the prestigious Commonwealth Club and Gymkhana Club.

Whenever he was able to come back to New Delhi, he tried to understand the social network of the company.

'Nothing better than being seen at the watering holes in the clubs,' one of the senior managers of his division told him.

Spending time at the clubs gave him an opportunity to get to know his colleagues, as well as young managers from other companies in New Delhi. Gulping down several glasses of the clubs' signature Bloody Marys accompanied by masala peanuts laced with green chillies and an abundant sprinkling of lemon, he started to understand the networking opportunities these evenings afforded him.

It was during one of these Saturday evenings that he was introduced to Lata. She was visiting the club with her parents and when he saw her, he realized it was love at first sight.

Lata was a fiercely independent young lady and had grown up in a very secure home. She never hesitated to speak her mind, unlike a lot of girls her age in the late seventies.

It was this quality, other than her looks, that endeared her to Rahul and they started going out. After the first few weeks, they realized that both of them had a future together. One evening, Rahul told Lata a little uncertainly, 'I think I am falling in love with you, Lata. I want to spend the rest of my life with you.'

'Think?' she remarked. 'You are not sure? It takes a lot of love to make a home and a household.'

Rahul let the moment pass and they kept dating. Neither of them was willing to raise the subject of marriage again. However, both of them recognized that they were still in love with each other. As they started to get more intimate, he tried to cross the threshold one late evening in his apartment. She stopped him just short of going all the way.

'This I will not allow,' she said, 'till we are married.'

Within six months of meeting her, he proposed and she accepted.

They were married a few months later in a simple ceremony.

Raj

From childhood, Raj Dhingra, born in 1955 in the city of Chandigarh, knew that he wouldn't become a doctor like his father.

Dr Jagdish Dhingra, MBBS, had struggled through his bachelor's degree in medicine. He built a small practice in the city from a clinic he started in the garage of his house soon after he had graduated. He didn't pursue further studies because he felt that there was no way he could gain admission into a master's degree programme for medicine. He continued to see his patients in the same garage till the day he died.

Dr Dhingra had no major ambitions and was happy with the twenty-odd patients he received every day. He had no qualms in selling the medicine samples given to him by medical representatives and closely monitored his share of revenue from the referrals he made for any additional tests to the local laboratory or imaging centre. He would collect all his fees and other earnings in cash and did not believe in paying taxes.

'Why should I pay taxes?' he would often say over dinner. 'Look at the condition of the roads and the infrastructure of the city. The government cannot give us regular power. I have to pay a bribe even to get gas.'

Growing up in such an environment, young Raj never

questioned his father's ethics. On the contrary, he started to accept that honesty was never black or white. It could be interpreted in several shades of grey. He saw his father's ability to earn money outside his practice as a virtue.

Dr Dhingra's ability of justifying 'shortcuts' and compromising on values would stay with his son all his life.

Raj was educated at a local public school and even when he was in class eleven, the final class, he was not sure of what he would do next. Since his primary education had been in Punjabi, he was never really able to make English his first language. More often than not, he thought in Punjabi and then literally translated his thoughts into English as he spoke. It was not unusual for him to talk about his 'extra-century' perception and despite being corrected several times, he continued to use this phrase throughout his life whenever he was asked about how he had figured out an answer to a tough question or situation. He recognized his lack of proper English education as a weakness, and worked hard at learning new phrases. He would use all these phrases whenever he wanted to demonstrate his knowledge of the language.

Raj had been introduced to the joys of smoking and drinking in the final years of school and became a chain smoker, at times lighting one cigarette with another. His yellow, nicotine-stained fingertips and nails were clear evidence of his addiction.

He had also started to enjoy alcohol after some friends got him to drink a bottle of cough syrup stolen from his father's clinic. When the cough syrup stopped giving him a high, he started to steal a few drinks from his father's cupboard at home.

The first time he came home drunk, his parents were shocked. His mother caught him by his ears and took him to the toilet. She made him throw up all the alcohol, then put him to bed, where he slept for over twenty hours.

This was the first time he had had one too many, but it would definitely not be the last.

He had no interest in taking up his father's profession and he certainly did not want to take over Dr Dhingra's small and inconsequential clinic. He knew that he would never be able to pass the pre-medical tests to qualify for a seat in any medical college. He also recognized that he would not be able to make it into the IITs, given his overall grades and his poor mathematical abilities.

Yet, Raj was very ambitious.

He wanted to go well beyond Chandigarh and make a mark on the national stage. He aspired to become a manager in a big company, where he would be able to throw his weight around, like he had seen in so many Bollywood movies. He remembered film dialogues and used some of the more catchy lines in his daily conversation.

'I am having a big ambition and I must become the top boss,' he would tell his friends.

He loved Bollywood movies and would see a film several times, until he had memorized all the dialogues. There was no movie he missed in the local cinema hall. He was particularly partial to Dev Anand.

'I get my money back the minute I see Dev Anand on the screen. After that it is profit for the next three hours,' he would say with a dreamy look in his eyes.

His favourite movie was *Deewar*, and he never tired of using the phrase '*Main pheke huye paise nahin uthata* (I don't pick up money that is thrown at me)' though he had always taken money from his father.

Following the example of a lot of other students in his

school, he applied to various colleges in New Delhi and was admitted to Hans Raj College in 1974 to pursue an honours degree in economics. His marks were not enough to get him an admission into either of the two premier institutions: St Stephen's or Hindu College.

The three years at college were pretty uneventful, lazing around in the college canteen and bunking classes to watch blue films in the apartment of one of his rich friends. When they had free time, Raj and his friends would often sit at a bus stop outside one of the women's colleges and ogle at the girls, grading their looks on a scale of one to ten.

Raj managed to pass his examinations using a 'kunji', a 'guide' containing a set of questions with suggested answers. Such books were easily available in all university bookstores. The authors of these best-selling books would 'predict and guess' the question paper of the forthcoming examinations by iterating the combination of questions in the previous years. Examination papers would normally have eight questions on different subjects and students were expected to answer five. Raj would prepare for three, in order to get a passing grade. Books were seldom read by him during the semester and it was not uncommon for his classmates to see him open a brand new textbook as the examination day drew close.

College was also the period when Raj was to discover his weakness for the fairer sex. He was introduced to the joys of easy sex by one of his seniors, who took him for a night out at GB Road, the red-light district of New Delhi. There, he lost his virginity in a hurried manner to a Nepali girl who could not have been more than sixteen, in a dark musty room on a dirty bed sheet.

The total money spent for this encounter was a princely

₹10, a fortune in the late seventies. The ease with which he was able to seek a release by paying money appealed to young Raj, and he often went back to the same girl during his years at college. For a short while, he almost believed that he had fallen in love with her, though this notion was negated by the young lady after each visit, as she performed her duties in a disinterested manner.

'*Paisa do aur aage badho. Agla grahak bahar khada hai. Jaldi karo, baboo.* (Pay the money and move on. The next customer is standing outside. Hurry up, sir),' she would tell him each time, hardly bothering to recognize her loyal and devoted customer.

Seeking out opportunities for paid sex to fulfill his physical needs would become a part of Raj's life in the future as well. Whichever part of India or the world he would travel to, he would call for escorts to his hotel room.

In the third year, faced with the prospect of life after college, he was once again confronted with what to do next. His parents were of no help to him at all. They had never seen life outside their small and restricted community. His father knew that his son would not join him in the clinic and once that was clear, he had no further inputs to give his son.

'Let him do what he wants. He has become too big for me,' his father would tell his mother. 'Besides, I don't even know what to advise him.'

Once again, Raj had no idea about what he wanted to do, so he drifted along with most of his friends. Everyone seemed to be applying for admission to an MBA degree. One of his close friends had an extra application form for the CAT exam for an MBA programme. Raj decided to fill the form and apply, without thinking what he would do next.

He worked through several multiple-choice tests in books

for the CAT. He had always been a quick thinker and once he figured out the methodology to answer these questions using the practice tests, he was able to complete them correctly and swiftly.

He managed to pass the written examinations for several management schools and in the interview process was lucky enough to be selected to the University of Chandigarh. He worked hard during his MBA programme, as he had started to understand the opportunities this education would afford him. At the end of his two-year programme he topped his class of fifty students.

His philosophy, defined in his words, was simply, 'If you can do, do. If you cannot, admit yourself.'

~

The HR managers of Trust Corporation normally visited the country's top business schools, and the Chandigarh business school where Raj was studying was on their list as well. Raj had topped his class and despite his below-average communication skills, the recruiting team recognized his intuitiveness, aggressiveness and freshness.

They decided to offer him a shot at the job in New Delhi. He was the only candidate to be selected as a management trainee from his class.

'My life has been swings and pendulums all the way through. From this side to that side all the time,' was Raj's answer every time he was asked about his background and his family.

His first assignment on completion of his twelve-month training was in the power division. The company's first power plant was in Himachal Pradesh, where they were setting up a large hydel power unit. This enabled Raj to travel via his hometown. He would take a train to Chandigarh and then a car from there up into the beautiful Himalayas.

Within a year of starting work, Raj was persuaded by his mother to get married. She selected a nice pretty young girl, the daughter of a wealthy landlord from their village in Punjab. The match would also bring a lot of dowry. After all, the Dhingras had invested so much money in educating their son.

Lovely, as the young lady was called, was barely nineteen years old and was a stereotypical bride from North Indian advertisements—'fair-complexioned, well-mannered, homemaker with the ability to cook tasty Punjabi food and capable of bearing many strong sons.' She was convent educated and spoke the Queen's English that most Indians claim to speak. For Lovely, getting married and settling down was what she had aspired for all her young life. For Lovely's parents, Raj was an ideal match since he was working with a 'multinational' company with 'good prospects for the future'.

Raj met Lovely only once at his parents' home and immediately gave his consent to the match.

'Achhi hai,' he said to his parents, undressing her with his eyes, looking lecherously and admiringly at her youthful body.

Though Lovely would have willingly given her consent to the marriage, she was never asked. Once the boy had said yes, the marriage was finalized.

Raj was later delighted to learn that Lovely was equally passionate about Hindi films as him. They spent several evenings watching movies together in various cinema halls in Chandigarh. Her favourite actor was Dev Anand as well. After going for an evening show, they would have some delicious chole bhature with a side order of chicken tikka in the shop outside the cinema hall. They would wind up their evening with a tall glass of sweet lassi.

Raj had wanted an undemanding wife who he could control and mould in his own manner, and Lovely fitted his requirement well.

~

Sangeeta

Sangeeta Malhotra was the youngest of the group of five trainees who joined Trust Corporation.

Born into an army officer's family in 1958, she had been given an upbringing no different from her older brother by her parents. From the beginning, she was a tomboy and spent most of her time with her brother's friends. Initially they indulged her and as she entered her teens, they encouraged her to spend more time with them.

Sangeeta was exceptionally beautiful, doe-eyed with well-defined features. Her chiselled face with high cheekbones and sharp features attracted every boy around her.

Girls in the late seventies had virtually no recourse in the event of an attempted molestation, and Sangeeta faced several instances of groping by many young men who claimed to be her brother's friends. However, she was a smart young girl who also knew how to use her charms to get whatever she wanted from the swooning boys in her school.

When Sangeeta was in class eleven, her father was posted to Allahabad, where they were allotted a house on the ramparts of the old fort, built on the confluence of the rivers Ganga, Jamuna and the mythical Saraswati. Life inside the fort, surrounded by young boys and girls of her age, was filled with late evening parties and sleepovers. There was also intense competition in her school and Sangeeta always topped her class.

She soon became particularly close to a neighbour's son, whose father was a junior commissioned officer. Much against her parents' wishes, she would always be seen spending time with him. They started to discover each other's bodies through simple touching and an occasional hurried kiss when no one was watching.

One weekend when her parents were travelling, she invited him over to her home late at night. She lost her virginity to him that night in her own bed. Both of them were inexperienced and fumbled through the motions of making love, their youthful bodies on fire. A few minutes later, he slipped out of her house.

Shortly thereafter, he slipped out of her life as well.

Later in life, she often wondered at how uneventful losing her virginity had been. She had read so much about the excitement of the event in various books. Her school friends used to talk in hushed tones about what they looked forward to on their first night. She was actually disappointed that nothing of that sort had happened during her first time. She wondered if she had selected the wrong man.

Sangeeta was a very selfish girl. She would throw a tantrum with her parents and her older brother whenever she needed anything and more often than not, she was given what she wanted. As the baby of the family, everyone indulged her to a fault. She had never been a person who clung to anyone or anything, because she had never learned to develop an emotional connect with anyone.

At the same time, she was an exceptional student. She wrote the Joint Entrance Exam (JEE) for the Indian Institutes of Technology and was selected into IIT Delhi.

Life at IIT settled into a routine of classes and partying. Sangeeta had always believed in working hard and playing hard. She was different from most other girls on campus, being seen more with boys than girls. Like in school, she continued to use her feminine skills at IIT to get what she wanted. She quickly acquired the reputation of being a 'tease'.

She loved to ride pillion on a two-wheeler, the preferred and most affordable vehicle for a college student in the late seventies. She made friends with any guy who had a Yezdi motorcycle or a Bajaj Chetak scooter. Unlike other girls who sat with both their legs on one side, she preferred to sit like a boy, straddling the bike, holding on to the driver's waist, her breasts pressed into his back, her hair open, flying wantonly in the air. This would drive the young men crazy. They were always looking for an opportunity to take her for a ride.

What Sangeeta did not realize was that teasing too many people too many times would prove to be dangerous.

In her final year at IIT she started seeing the college hunk Arvind on a regular basis. His brand-new Yezdi motorcycle, which he had rebranded as 'ipzeY' by unscrewing and turning around the logo on the fuel tank, was a major reason.

One Christmas Eve, she agreed to go out with him for a late-night party. She wore a pair of black leather trousers and a warm leather jacket, with a skimpy top underneath. She eagerly jumped on to the motorcycle, sitting in her usual fashion.

As they drove past the deeply forested Ridge, often called the lungs of Delhi, which was always a very quiet and lonely place, he stopped on the pretext of having run out of petrol. She did not realize that they had stopped very strategically opposite the gates of the garden, the same area where the infamous 'Billa–Ranga' crime had taken place in 1978.

They went inside the garden and before she could realize what was happening, Arvind was all over her, trying to hug and kiss her. This came as a complete shock. She tried to resist but he was far too strong for her. With one hand on her mouth to muffle her screams, he pushed her on to a park bench and unzipped her leather jacket. He tore open her top and forced her leather trousers down. With a quickness that surprised her, he entered her violently. His eyes opened wide as he realized that she was not a virgin. A few moments later, he had finished and without another look at her, he zipped his trousers and walked off, leaving her sobbing in the middle of the dark park, with one last comment, 'That is what you get for teasing me and the other boys.'

Sangeeta knew her life had changed irretrievably. But there was no point in getting angry or crying over spilt milk. She also recognized that she would not get justice from a male-dominated society.

She gathered herself and managed to get an autorickshaw back to the college campus. The rickshaw driver looked at her strangely as she came out of the garden but did not ask any questions. She did not run into anyone on the campus since everybody seemed to be out partying.

Once in her room, she rushed into the shower, trying to wash away the incident.

Life at IIT would no longer be the same. Sangeeta went through the last six months mechanically, like a zombie, though she did not compromise on her study schedule and ended up once again at the top of her class.

~

Sangeeta did not apply to any of the top MBA schools in India, since she wanted to leave her memories behind and run away from the country. She applied to business schools in USA and was selected to Harvard Business School on a full scholarship, which she gratefully accepted. Without waiting for her graduation ceremony she left Indian shores, hoping that she would never have to come back to the country where she had been violated.

While doing her MBA programme, Sangeeta applied for US citizenship. Seeing her academic record, her application was fast-tracked and she got it easily. Since India did not permit dual citizenship, she was required to surrender her Indian citizenship before she accepted the other. It took her no time to surrender her Indian passport at the Indian Embassy and take the oath to become a US citizen.

~

The late seventies was a period when most of the developed world was in the throes of a major recession, as a result of the oil crisis in 1973 and the energy crisis in 1979. Unemployment rates had touched record levels in the US. During Sangeeta's years at Harvard, the US economy was going through a severe contraction and most of her seniors found it difficult to get decent jobs after graduation.

In 1980, when she was to graduate, there were no jobs for foreign students in USA that she would have liked, so when some Indian friends sent her the advertisement for Trust Corporation, she decided to apply.

She had no idea that she would be selected. Since she had no other job offers in hand, she had no option but to accept the offer and return to India to face her ghosts once more.

On joining her new job with Trust Corporation and

completing her first-year training, given her background as an engineer and a Harvard graduate, Sangeeta was assigned to the newly formed software division of the company.

This was a new area of business in India and like some of the major Indian companies, the board of directors of Trust Corporation had also decided that they would like to seen at the forefront of technology, even though they recognized internally that what they were really starting off with was body shopping. No one on the board knew what to expect, but they were driven by the need to make correct statements for the political establishment.

In the year she joined the company, the software business was the theme of the chairman's annual communication to the shareholders. Seeing the importance of her business group, Sangeeta knew that her career had got off to a flying start.

~

Sangeeta's parents were keen to get her married once she started working but she was not interested, given her experience with men in college and her intense desire to win in the corporate world. She had never been able to forget how she had been violated by a guy whom she had trusted and that incident had left her with a deep dislike of any man touching her or even coming close to her.

However, she recognized that socially, a single woman would get a lot of people talking and the average Indian male would always see her as 'easy picking'. So she relented when her mother put pressure on her for marriage.

Her parents found a young army major, Ajay Sharma, from the same corps as her father. His parents and her parents were friends and as families, they had spent a lot of time together.

Sangeeta's parents were simple retired army people and had absolutely no idea about what their daughter had been through in college. They had always known that their daughter was ambitious but like all Indian parents, they had assumed that she would also settle down and give them grandchildren.

In her very first meeting with Major Ajay Sharma, she told him, 'I will marry you because of the pressure from my parents, but for me, my career is of prime importance. There has been a lot of uncertainty in my life with all the transfers my father had in the army. So I will not move with you wherever you are transferred. We will maintain separate homes. But we will make every effort to try and spend as much time as possible with each other.'

She had thought this would throw him off. Ajay, on the other hand was quite smitten with her confidence, her educational background and her beauty. A straightforward and direct-talking army officer who had always been taught to believe in the goodness of people, Major Sharma thought that he would be able to change his wife-to-be's thinking once they were married.

'We are living in the eighties, Sangeeta,' he said. 'I expect you to work and build a career for yourself.'

'I will also retain my maiden name,' she said, hoping he would not counter with the suggestion that she call herself Sangeeta Malhotra Sharma, as was the trend. She was pleasantly surprised when he accepted immediately.

'What's in a name?' he replied. 'You can call yourself what you want.'

'I will also have no time for children,' she further added, pushing her luck with him. Ajay frowned, shook his head and said, 'Why don't we discuss this after we have spent some time together?'

To which she responded, 'I think it is better to clarify all our points before we get married.'

She was pleasantly surprised to see him agree to this request as well without saying anything.

Sangeeta thought that Ajay had accepted all her conditions and Ajay assumed that she would change once they were married. He would realize later in life what a strong-willed woman she was. Each time he would try to raise the matter of living together or having children, she would remind him in no uncertain terms about their understanding.

They were married in the local gurdwara. This was followed by the customary ceremonies at home. Both sets of parents hosted a grand reception for all their friends and family, where Sangeeta stood dutifully next to her husband. Everyone who met them wanted a photograph with the newly-weds and commented, 'What a lovely couple they make! Sangeeta is looking so beautiful.'

Since Major Sharma was posted in a sensitive area of Kashmir, he needed prior approval of the Indian Army before taking his wife to the location. He was shocked to learn that Sangeeta was a US citizen. No one had told him about this before. He was aware that the army would never give him permission to take his wife to sensitive areas.

When he asked Sangeeta about it, she replied, 'You never asked me. Anyway, what is the big deal about my citizenship?'

'You will never get approval from the Indian Army to live with me in sensitive areas and the army will always look at me with suspicion,' Ajay said angrily.

'There is not much I can do about my citizenship, can I?' she replied. 'If I cannot visit you in your home, you can come and visit me in my home in New Delhi.'

He had no choice but to accept this as a fait accompli. They had started off their newly-wedded life on the wrong note. While on one hand he was worried about his marriage, he was equally concerned about how this development would affect his career.

However, for Sangeeta, her American citizenship had come as a blessing in disguise. Ajay would not be able to force her to live with him.

Within a couple of days after their wedding, even before the mehndi on her hands had faded, she took a flight back to New Delhi, leaving Ajay to return to his army unit in Srinagar a few days later.

She promised him that she would take more time off from her work later in the year, so that they could go for their honeymoon.

~

Iqbal

From childhood, Iqbal Mohammad was used to seeing large stacks of cash in his house. His conservative Muslim family, who lived in Lucknow, was in the carpets business and had their weaving mills in Bhadohi, Uttar Pradesh. They had built a huge empire of carpet manufacturing and trading, and real estate. The carpet business was sustained on the young fingers of minor workers who would weave excellent carpets that were sold to the ever hungry markets of the Western world. The real-estate business was built through milking their minority status, which enabled the family to get strong political patronage. They were able to buy land wherever they wanted at low prices simply because they had the ability to swing the minority vote in favour of the local politician.

The youngest of five brothers, Iqbal was born in 1956. His eldest brother was twenty years older than him, so he was always the baby of the family.

In both the family businesses, transactions were done primarily in cash. Carpet buyers would come from overseas and leave US dollars. They would then ask for the invoices of the carpets to be significantly lower than the actual price. This suited Iqbal's family, since they got to pay lower income tax. At the same time, the real-estate business in India needed a lot of money. Iqbal's family used the income generated from the carpets to buy large tracts of land at low prices.

Iqbal never questioned any of these business practices because he assumed that his elders were doing the right thing and as long as he was able to spend on whatever he wanted, who was he to question the source of these funds?

The family also donated cash lavishly in the local elections to all major political contenders, thus hedging their bets, though they always stayed away from direct attention and did not ever contemplate contesting elections themselves. In addition, they donated liberally to the various shrines and temples in and around their area of business.

'Why fight an election,' his father would say, 'when you can fund a politician and get him to do what you need?'

Iqbal was sent to the prestigious La Martiniere College for Boys in Lucknow when he was five years old, a school that started functioning on 1 October 1845. Its students were very proud of the fact that their school had participated in the Revolt of 1857 and that it was the only school in the country which had been presented colours bearing the legend 'Defence of Lucknow 1857'.

Iqbal had been taught to say his prayers five times a day and though he was not always able to comply with his teachings, he made it a point to pray at least once at the appointed hour. He was also very particular about fasting during the holy month of Ramzan, and La Martiniere always made arrangements to serve him tea and biscuits before dawn and a warm meal after sunset. His religious bent of mind stayed with him all his life.

Since his parents and older brothers never let him feel that he was short of cash and his mother ensured a steady supply of rich and delicious food, Iqbal became the darling of all his classmates and seniors.

School life was quite uneventful barring one incident, which scarred him for life. When Iqbal was in class seven, an older boy in his class took a particular liking to him. He would show Iqbal pictures of nude girls and give him pornographic books. Iqbal had never seen or read such stuff before and he started hanging out with the older boy regularly. Both of them used to sit on the last bench in class.

During one class, the boy put his hand on Iqbal's thigh under the table. He started to caress Iqbal's thigh and every once in a while, his fingertips would reach Iqbal's groin and then teasingly move back to his thigh. Iqbal was surprised at the way his body responded to the boy's touch. He loved the tingling sensation in his groin. This seemingly innocent touching got bolder and continued for a few weeks with absolutely no discouragement from Iqbal. One day, in the middle of a mathematics class, the boy unbuttoned Iqbal's trousers, put his hand inside his underwear and started to fondle him. Within a few seconds, Iqbal felt intense warmth and pleasure.

Iqbal had never felt such intense passion within him. In grateful response he reached out and squeezed the other boy's thigh.

The boy started to take more liberties in the following weeks and Iqbal allowed him to do so.

One evening after dinner, he took Iqbal to an abandoned toilet on the school campus, all the while caressing and exciting him.

'Take off your trousers and I will show you some new tricks,' he said. Iqbal did so willingly.

'Now turn around and face the platform.' By the time Iqbal realized what was happening, the boy had undone his pants and dropped them to the ground.

Iqbal was forcibly made to face the wall, bending over a

cement platform with a dirty sink. He protested vigorously and violently but the boy was far too strong for him.

'Stop, stop! What are you doing!' Iqbal shouted. When he did not get a response, he cried, 'Please let me go. I will do whatever else you want me to...'

With his face on the cement platform and his hands pinned on either side, Iqbal could not move. His underwear was pulled down forcibly and he felt his friend applying some greasy substance on his anus. Then he felt a searing pain, so intense that he passed out.

When he regained consciousness a few seconds later, his hands were free. He looked back to see the other boy pulling up his trousers and walking away. With shivering hands, Iqbal wiped away the traces of semen and blood and pulled up his trousers. He was even more embarrassed to see that he'd had an orgasm too.

He knew that he had made a grave error by going with this boy and stayed away from him for the rest of his years at school. Deep in his heart, though, he also realized that he had enjoyed the physical contact.

Since Iqbal felt that he had committed a grave sin, he chose to keep quiet about this incident.

When he finished his intermediate examination in 1974, like every graduating schoolboy, he chiselled his name and the year of his graduation in bold letters for posterity on the long stone steps in front of the impressive school building. The school steps had names chiselled on them over the years and it was not unusual to find a former student walking up and down the steps looking for his name.

Meanwhile, unknown to Iqbal, the family business had been declining rapidly. Products made by minors were no longer finding favour in a more aware Western world and the market for expensive hand-knotted carpets was being taken over by cheaper machine-made carpets. The land owned by the family had been pledged to banks to raise more money for the carpet business and since no returns were coming in, the banks had foreclosed their loans and taken over most of their real estate.

The dire financial situation of the family came as a surprise and shock to Iqbal. He had to quickly adjust to the fact that his planned life of luxury in a family business run by his older brothers had come to naught, and that he would have to stand on his own feet.

He had always been a very short-tempered person and on receiving this news, he was very angry with his parents. He blamed the loss of his family fortune on his brothers who, he believed, had led a lifestyle beyond their means and frittered away the family wealth. However, there was nothing he could do.

Encouraged by his father to chart out a career on his own, Iqbal decided to pursue a course in chartered accountancy and simultaneously attain a degree in commerce. He started earning a paltry ₹100 a month as an articled clerk with a local chartered accountancy firm as well.

The shock of the collapse of the family business and the intense anger he felt for his family built a strong desire within him to succeed at all costs and made him burn the midnight oil. He topped his commerce examination and managed to pass all his CA examinations in his first attempt as well. He had an excellent mind for numbers. By the time he was twenty-two years old, he had qualified as a chartered accountant.

Armed with his CA and an honours degree in commerce, he confidently applied to Trust Corporation for a job in their finance department and was selected to join their batch of management trainees. Unknown to him, however, his father had also called in past favours from a political contact and asked him to have a word with the chairman about his son's selection.

Like most business organizations in India, political influence could not be wished away and the chairman was obliged to respect the request being made by the politician.

Trust Corporation had always valued its finance managers and significantly empowered them. Finance professionals in the company had a strong dotted-line relationship with the finance director, who saw himself as the mentor and guide of all finance managers in the group.

On completion of his management training, Iqbal was appointed as an assistant manager in the corporate finance department at the head office in New Delhi.

~

Coming from a very traditional Lucknawi family who blamed God and the law for the financial state they were in after the failure of their business, Iqbal had been brought up with orthodox thoughts and beliefs about religion, life, families, women and children.

'Allah has punished our family for all the black money we made, as well as for all the carpets we got woven by young children,' his mother would often tell his father, who had no way to counter this allegation made by his wife.

Iqbal had never considered the possibility of dating any young ladies. He had refused to go to school socials where girls from other schools would come. La Martiniere was an all boys' school, and his college and CA degrees were completed under the watchful eye of his stern mother. He was shy and not wont to going out and making friends with anyone, leave alone the fairer sex. His violation by another boy added to his hesitation in making new friends.

Many young Indians live sheltered lives and are not encouraged to mix freely with the opposite sex. Consequently they are protected from the business of 'falling in love', which can lead to all sorts of heartaches, clouded judgment, unsuitable relationships and tragic consequences.

Iqbal simply assumed that his parents would find a suitable match for him, as was the practice in his family. He had been taught that marriages were always 'made in heaven' between 'soulmates' destined for each other.

Though his family had a certain status in society because of their background, they were no longer wealthy, so other well-to-do families with eligible daughters refused Iqbal's marriage proposal. His parents finally found a bride, Samina, for him from within their community. Samina was a beautiful girl from an average middle-class family. His 'nikah' was conducted without his ever having met the bride prior to it.

Iqbal resented the fact that he had not received any dowry from Samina's family. When he thought of all the gold, land, cars and cash his family had received during his brothers' weddings, he was filled with anger towards his bride.

Samina would have to answer to him all her life for this lack of dowry.

The wedding celebrations were very quiet; nothing compared to the three-day lavish wedding parties for his brothers. Iqbal recognized the need for austerity given the financial situation of his family but still resented the fact that the arrangements for his marriage had been an apology compared to the former celebrations. However, he chose to keep this anger bottled up inside him.

Anita

Anita Fernandes was born in 1956 into a very conservative Christian family. Hers was a joint family household full of bureaucrats who had spent a lifetime with the government pushing files. Her father was an officer in the Indian Administrative Service. She was surrounded by uncles and aunts who worked in the defence services, police, railways and banks. Everyone expected her to follow the family tradition and take the entrance examination for the Indian Civil Services. But Anita had seen so much bureaucracy that she had made up her mind to not even attempt a career with the government.

Anita was sent to an all girls' school when she was five years old. On one of her visits back home in the summer vacations, when she was barely nine, she was sexually abused by an older cousin who threatened her with dire consequences if she told anyone. She could not really remember later in life what had happened between the two of them, except that what she had been asked to do was incorrect, because of the secrecy associated with it. She lived with the guilt all her life, not knowing who to discuss this with, for fear of a strong reprisal.

Anita had a very low threshold for physical pain and each time she fell down and hurt herself, she would bring the house down. If she had a fever, she needed all her family around her to pamper her and make her feel important.

Her parents kept a very strict vigil on her and she was never allowed to go for dates with boys, unlike her classmates. Parties at the club or Sunday movies were permitted, but her mother was always close at hand.

Anita's mother was a deeply religious person who never missed church, and she made it a point to take Anita to the church every Sunday without fail. Anita, like her mother, started using the church as a crutch for everything. Her church visits were to become a regular feature for life. She never used any foul language and even words like 'damn' and 'bloody' were not in her lexicon.

She was a good student in school and her grades normally kept her in the top three in her class. On completing school, she got admission into Miranda House, Delhi University, once again an all girls' college. During her three years there, she was always dropped off by car and picked up from the college gates every evening. The thought of bunking college and going for a movie with her friends never crossed her mind. She was happy in her world, with her family and God.

Anita applied for the MBA admission tests in 1977 and was selected by Xavier Labour Relations Institute (XLRI), which enabled her to specialize in human resources, a career which seemed to have been custom-made for her. She was able to empathize with people and relate to their issues without ever getting agitated or angry.

When Trust Corporation visited XLRI campus for recruitments, she was a natural choice, since she had also interned with the company after her first year at business school. She was near the top of her class and her communication skills were excellent.

What she would never know was that Trust was also very conscious of gender balance in the company. Therefore, they had taken an internal decision that the trainee they hired for human resources would have to be a woman, given that they had already selected three other men and one woman.

On completion of the management training programme, Anita was assigned to the HR department.

Her first posting was at the corporate head office in New Delhi.

~

As a child, Anita had a crush on a very handsome Anglo-Indian boy, Michael, who was ten years older than her. He was tall and played the Spanish guitar. He was also able to sing songs by Lobo and Cliff Richards, which endeared him to the fun-loving community he lived in.

Michael was the local hero for all young boys and girls in the community. He was the boy every girl wanted to dance with at the church parties and whom every girl wanted to date at the school social.

Michael had never really focused on completing his education and had dropped out after completing Senior Cambridge. However, he always seemed to have plenty of money, which he earned by doing odd jobs and cheating people whenever he got an opportunity. He would take a foreign couple to show them the sights of Delhi and happily chauffeur an old lady for a dinner party. He would fix television antennas on rooftops and supervise the painting in someone's home. No job was too small, as long as he was able to earn money.

'I work to earn more money, man,' he would say. 'I don't care what the work is or who gives it to me.'

He used to ride a powerful 350-CC Royal Enfield 'Bullet' motorcycle wearing a dark brown leather jacket. He generally had a pretty young girl behind him and this image became a powerful source of attraction for Anita. Every time she saw him from a distance, she wished she was on the seat behind him. The powerful motorcycle with its deep bass thud from the engine would make her yearn to touch him, and she could feel a weakness in her knees.

Michael was always surrounded by beautiful girls and there were times when Anita felt very jealous. He knew of her crush on him and loved the attention he got from her, but he chose to maintain a distance from Anita, knowing full well that he could have her at any time.

Michael had followed her education closely and knew that this young girl was destined to go places in the corporate world once she had been admitted into her MBA programme.

When Anita returned in the vacations, he started to pay extra attention to her. Though she too had always maintained a steady distance from Michael, both of them had stayed in touch.

Soon after she started working at Trust Corporation, Michael, whose career was not going anywhere in particular, given his lack of education and his desire for an easy life with little or no work, realized that Anita could be his meal ticket for the rest of his life.

He turned on all his charms when he first walked up to her and asked her to be his date at the community dance hall for the Christmas party. She was swept off her feet by him and willingly agreed. That evening was wonderful and he was at his charming best. He spent every minute of the evening with her and even when he was approached by other girls for a dance, he refused. He made her promise that she would be his date for the New Year party a few days later.

He kissed her for the first time at the New Year party. She loved the soft warm touch of his lips on hers.

Over the next few months, they started to meet every evening and go everywhere together. He would never let her pay for anything and she was very impressed with his constant supply of money for both of them.

Anita had shared with Michael that she was a virgin and that she had been waiting for the right person to come along. Though she would have readily given herself completely to him any evening, he decided that she was far too precious to be treated like most other girls, where his only objective had been to take them to bed.

Within a few months of going out regularly, he knew it was time to ask her the question she had been waiting for.

'Will you marry me?'

'Yes,' Anita said immediately, without a second thought or doubt in her mind.

They decided to seek the blessings of their parents for an early wedding. Since both of them were Roman Catholics and their parents went to the same church, they did not face any resistance from the families.

Anita and Michael were married by their local pastor at a simple but elegant ceremony, which was followed by much singing, dancing, drinking and eating.

Anita thought that she must be the luckiest and happiest girl in the world.

~

The First Decade

The 1980s were marked by the date 31 October 1984—a dark day in India's history, when Prime Minister Indira Gandhi was assassinated by her own bodyguards.

At the same time, Rajiv Gandhi's ascension to the role of prime minister when he was only forty years old filled the country with hope and energy. He was seen by the youth as a clean politician and they took his promise of a corruption-free India to heart. Youngsters thronged to his meetings and lined the roads when his motorcade drove past. He represented their dream of an India that would stride towards the comity of nations in the world as an equal partner.

His leading the Congress to an unprecedented victory with almost 80 per cent of the members of Parliament was seen by the youth as the positive signal they had been waiting for. Years of poor government policies had stifled their creative energy and they hoped to see some decisive leadership that would pull the country out of its sleepy Hindu rate of growth.

However, that was not to be. The Rajiv Gandhi government stumbled from one scandal to another and in mid-1987, the Bofors scandal destroyed the image of the dynamic young prime minister. The youth abandoned him and the Congress party suffered a humiliating defeat in the 1989 elections.

~

Meanwhile, life had just begun for Rahul, Raj, Sangeeta, Iqbal and Anita. They were all appointed as assistant managers on completion of their management training programme.

Each one of them was determined to run faster than the others to get ahead in the race to the top job and stake a claim to the corner office.

They travelled together and stayed in the same hotels. They shared every meal and the bonds between them started to get stronger.

The others realized that they should leave Iqbal alone when he was in a foul mood, since no one wanted to hear his raving and ranting.

Raj had to be avoided after he'd had his third drink of the evening. Once he had crossed his threshold, he would become over-friendly with ladies and have no hesitation in touching them.

Each time Sangeeta would start talking about her ambition and predict when she would occupy the corner office, the rest would walk away.

Whenever Anita would start talking about the role of Christ in her life, they would roll their eyes and say 'not again'.

Throughout the year, the one sane voice was that of Rahul. He kept the group together and managed the internal conflicts amongst his friends by saying, 'Let's keep moving ahead, guys. We have our whole lives to compete with one another. Let us enjoy this one year we have together.'

While the two girls, Sangeeta and Anita, did spend a lot of time together, both of them became close to Rahul. The other two, Raj and Iqbal, were essentially loners, though they tried to be friendly. Therefore they gravitated towards each other though they had little in common.

After the first year they got busy with their separate functions and did not have enough time to catch up, other than hurried greetings in the corridors of the office. At the same time, they were also working hard to build relationships with senior colleagues in their respective business groups.

~

It was Trust Corporation's policy to provide accommodation to all its managers.

The original policy, written in the early part of the twentieth century, when the company had a lot of expatriate managers, stated that young managers were to be provided fully-furnished apartments. They were expected to move into their homes with only a toothbrush and their personal belongings. Over the years, the company had sustained this practice for each successive batch of management graduates.

All five assistant managers were given two-bedroom accommodations in various residential localities in New Delhi.

Their homes were furnished with basic requirements—a sofa set with side tables, a double bed, two single beds, a dining table with six chairs and two writing tables in each bedroom. In addition, they were given soft furnishings like curtains, bed sheets, towels and table linen. Finally, as part of their entitlement was a complete set of kitchen utensils, crockery and cutlery for six people and even table napkins.

As they progressed in their careers, they would be entitled to more perquisites like cars, refrigerators, air conditioners and other white goods. The number of air conditioners they would get depended entirely on their seniority. It was not uncommon among managers of the company, driven largely by their spouses, to compare notes on such assets.

While the number of company-owned assets was standard for each management level with no deviation permitted, proximity to the HR manager responsible for procurement ensured whether or not the brand of the given air conditioner was better.

Since all five were married by the time they finished their training, the assistant managers moved into their new homes with their respective spouses. There were two exceptions—Raj Dhingra, who had chosen to leave his wife with his parents in Chandigarh, and Sangeeta Malhotra, who had chosen to live in a separate home to pursue her independent career.

~

Rahul

Married life was wonderful for Rahul and Lata in the first two years. They spent a lot of time discussing their future and their life together.

'I have to head this company before I am fifty, Lata,' Rahul would tell her very often.

Lata would listen to him patiently. She rarely commented on his work, though she made it a point to say, 'You have my full support, Rahul. I know you can do it. But remember that you must balance your work and our life together. We have to build a strong home for ourselves and for our children later.'

Rahul would nod his head seriously and agree.

He would also discuss his colleagues, specifically sharing his views about his four peers.

'Sangeeta is ambitious and I need to watch out for her'; 'Raj is the dark horse. I shouldn't underestimate him'; 'Iqbal has a strange streak that worries me. He may not be good for the company'; 'I am not worried about Anita. She is too meek and soft.'

Work pressure at the office had not yet picked up and Rahul was able to leave the office at a reasonable hour. He would be home in time to go out with Lata most evenings. Their social life was wonderful and Rahul's colleagues made extra efforts to welcome them. Rahul and Lata were seen as a bright young couple who met all the 'requirements' of the company. In addition to their friends from the office, Rahul also had a large circle of friends from his management school. So Rahul and Lata were never short of company. They regularly entertained at their home and were invited to other friends' homes as well. Weekends were spent lazing around the house, or in the more familiar surroundings of their club with selected friends and colleagues.

Lata was fully involved in Rahul's corporate and social life and was an excellent hostess. She was liked by the spouses of all his senior colleagues. Being accepted socially was a big positive for any young couple and very soon, Rahul and Lata were on the invitation list of the chairman and other directors. Raj, Iqbal and Sangeeta resented that they were not invited to these dos, but there was nothing they could do about it.

Lata was as ambitious as Rahul for his career and she would go out of her way to meet with the spouses of senior management. Trust Corporation had always encouraged couples to take an active interest not only in the work of the company, but also in the social and extra-curricular activities organized outside office hours.

As a manager in the highly profitable alcohol division, young Rahul was put through his paces and required to travel quite extensively. He was being groomed for senior management and therefore, he had to visit the markets, meet the distributors, visit the company's factories, understand the alcohol production techniques and learn how to 'nose' the products.

Lata's strong will power and the difference in their outlook to life was what kept their marriage going. Both were willing to make adjustments in their lives. Despite work pressure, they managed to take holidays together and visited their parents once every year. Lata had been a brilliant student and it was easy for her to find a job in the local college. Most of the students in her class were only a few years younger than her.

Over the next three years, they had two children, a son and a daughter, and they knew that their family was complete.

~

In later years, Rahul worked round the clock to move ahead in his corporate career. He knew that the first ten years would make all the difference between him and his peers. Being away from home for several weeks at a stretch didn't really bother him.

However, his family life suffered. He was never able to make it to his children's school for the monthly parent-teacher meetings and he was travelling each time there was a function in school. He missed his son's first football match and his daughter's first piano recital. He was not there to celebrate when his son got the highest marks in mathematics or when his daughter read out her first poem. He missed holding his children's hands when they were unwell and he was never at home to tuck them into bed or read to them. He realized he was missing out on some important moments, but justified it by thinking it was all for their future.

When his son showed him a Lego set he had built, Rahul simply said, 'Very nice, beta. Now go away and play because Papa is working.' When his daughter came to give him a card she had made for him for Father's Day, he put the card in his briefcase without noticing the tears in his daughter's eyes.

In order to make up for his long absences, he would buy expensive gifts for the children and Lata each time he returned from his travels. He knew that he was buying peace at home and deep down he recognized that gifts were no real substitute for spending time with them.

'Look what Papa has brought for you,' he would yell each time he came home. However, he failed to notice that the excitement the children showed dulled over the years and there were several 'guilt presents' that lay unopened in their cupboards.

He tried to be a good father by taking his children out on the weekends he was home, even though he was very tired. Very often, he would return late on Friday night from a business trip and leave on a Sunday evening for an early morning meeting in Mumbai or Chennai, but he would try his best to spend time with his family too.

When he reflected on his own childhood, Rahul remembered with a lot of fondness the time his father had spent with him, working on his mathematics and physics problems. He would recall the special moments of sharing his grades with his father. When his grades were good, he was always rewarded. When they were not good, his father encouraged him by saying, 'Are you satisfied that you have done your best? If yes, then you will do well next time.' He could never remember being chastised by his father for poor grades.

Rahul knew that he was not giving the same amount of time to his children. But he rationalized this by telling himself that his father had been far less ambitious and less successful than him.

It became a major point of argument between Lata and Rahul. In all their arguments, he always tried to reason, saying, 'Why do you think I am doing all this work, Lata? It is for you and the children and for us to have a good life.'

He never understood her answer, which was consistent.

'I don't want you to work so hard for me. I don't want anything material from you or your company. All that I want is for you to spend more time with me and your children.'

When he protested, 'But I am doing all this for you and for our home', her response was simply, 'Don't fool yourself Rahul.

'What you are doing in your company is only for yourself,' Lata would continue. 'You are ambitious and want to reach the top for yourself. Don't ever forget that and don't live under any misconception that you are doing this for us. While we will always support you in your career and hope that you realize your dreams, please remember that your children and I would be equally happy if you did not have such lofty ambitions.'

~

Rahul was very passionate about his work and loved every challenge that was presented to him.

He was an excellent worker, never afraid to take on additional jobs. It was not long before he started to get noticed by his seniors in the alcohol division and brought into strategy sessions. His quick understanding and excellence with numbers made him an integral part of most meetings.

The alcohol business has always had the best price laddering in the world. They have a product for every price segment and every customer, and therefore the pricing of the products is always kept very secret. Rahul started to get exposure to this critical aspect of the business.

In addition to the brands, he was also exposed to the various types of alcohol that his company manufactured.

He was sent to the corporate headquarters of the company in USA to train with his counterparts there. His first ever trip to the States was fascinating; he saw the wonderful land of opportunity that he had heard of so often from his seniors at IIT. After spending a month there, he returned even more committed to his company and determined that he would be the person from his batch to make a mark.

He dutifully purchased some clothes for Lata and toys for the children. On returning, he had to carefully calculate his expenses and return the excess foreign exchange left over from the trip. India, in the eighties, had draconian foreign exchange laws, and the possession of even five dollars could be seen as a violation of the Foreign Exchange Regulation Act, leading to a non-bailable arrest warrant.

Rahul was always very loyal to his company and would get into long arguments whenever someone raised the subject of the negative aspects of alcohol.

'Someone else will make the alcohol if we don't. At least with Trust Corporation you have the assurance of quality, and no spurious product from us will ever reach the market. Besides, it is a well-established medical fact that two drinks a day are actually good for you. In addition, alcohol can improve the mood, enhance relaxation and aid sleep,' he would opine, ignoring the problems of alcohol addiction that were so rampant.

As with any other addictive product, alcohol too offered an opportunity to make large profits. With growing income levels in the country, Trust Corporation had ambitious plans to launch its international brands at higher prices and earn higher profit margins.

Rahul moved up the hierarchy of the company quickly in the first decade, from management trainee to assistant manager to manager to senior manager within a short period. His growth within the alcohol division was seen as unprecedented. He was often referred to by his peers as the 'blue-eyed boy' of the director-in-charge.

Raj, Sangeeta, Iqbal and Anita were following his progress keenly, as he was theirs. All of them seemed to be on the fast track in their respective businesses or functions.

They knew that, like in any long race or marathon, the first ten years would give them similar growth opportunities. This period would be the time to pace one another and run together, testing the stamina of the others. It was in the second and third decades where the winner would begin to pull ahead.

The important thing to remember in any race, including the one in the corporate world, was to have the stamina to keep running at a steady pace, keep breathing normally and not panic, hold one's head high and do the right things.

~

Raj

Raj and Lovely were married in Chandigarh.

The wedding ceremonies lasted three days and their relatives from all over Punjab came for the celebrations. Like all Punjabi weddings, there was much singing and dancing and loud celebrations. Lovely's parents had given a generous dowry, which Raj's parents proudly displayed to all. Lovely's parents had, after all, managed to snag a son-in-law in a good profession for their daughter. Now they had to ensure that they buy happiness for her for the rest of her life. Gifts would continue to be sent to Raj's family as long as they lived.

Since Raj was required to travel extensively he decided that Lovely should stay in Chandigarh under the watchful eyes of his mother who, like most Indian mothers, supported the decision of her son.

'It is our duty to look after our parents, Lovely,' Raj explained to her. 'Besides, my work requires me to travel extensively and you will be very lonely in a company apartment in New Delhi.'

'But I want to be with you, ji,' she said. 'How can we build our home if we live separately?'

'You are only three hours away from Delhi and can come any time. In any case, I will be here every weekend with you,' Raj replied persuasively.

Lovely reluctantly agreed. She was equally ambitious for him and wanted to see her husband succeed. However, what Lovely had not bargained for was living away from her husband for the rest of her life.

Lovely settled into her routine of looking after her in-laws and Raj went back to work. Every weekend he would visit his family, arriving on a Friday evening and leaving on a Monday morning. Lovely was happy with these weekly conjugal visits and Raj was happy that his parents were being looked after. Whenever Raj was in Chandigarh, he made it a point to go for a movie with Lovely. She would look forward to these evenings, though there was not much he discussed other than the movie they had just seen.

Within two years of marriage, Lovely had given birth to two sons, which made both sets of parents and their extended families very happy.

Raj had not been present when his first son was born. He promised Lovely that he would make it up to her and their son.

When Lovely was expecting their second child, Raj had planned to be in Chandigarh for her delivery. However, when he received the message that the baby was due any day, he realized that he would not be able to go because of his work commitments. Instead of telling Lovely this, he kept quiet and arrived one day after the baby was born.

'Lovely, I'm so sorry. I was asked by my boss to finish some very urgent work and missed my flight,' he lied.

She was too tired to argue with him.

As the years passed, Lovely, due to indiscriminate eating and complete lack of exercise, put on a lot of weight. Raj did not like a fat wife in bed and soon started to lose interest in her. His conjugal visits stopped. Now, when he came to Chandigarh, his primary focus was on eating and drinking with the family and spending every night in a drunken stupor. He no longer reached out to hold Lovely, even as she craved his touch.

'You should join a gym to lose some weights,' he would tell her often.

~

From his college days Raj had developed an appetite for regular sex and had got used to paying for it whenever he needed it. Since he was not attracted to his wife any longer, he was always looking for opportunities. After one of his frustrating visits to Chandigarh, Raj succumbed to temptation in his office. He had his first affair with his secretary Barbara.

Barbara was a smart Anglo-Indian girl, who usually wore short skirts and high heels. She was in awe of Raj. In him, she saw an ambitious jet-setting boss who lived alone in a beautiful company apartment. She was aware that he was married but she assumed that Raj and his wife were estranged, since she had never seen the two of them together. She had never even seen her boss communicate with his wife, barring the monthly remittance of money.

'Would you like to have me for dinner this evening, Barbara?' Raj asked her one morning.

Barbara was taken aback by this sudden request, but composed herself and agreed, asking, 'But what is the occasion?'

'Not occasion at all. Just I am very lonely at home and bored in evening so thought I would ask you. I will pick you from your house at 7 p.m.,' he replied.

Raj was the perfect gentleman that evening. He and Barbara dined together at Kwality's Restaurant in Connaught Place and when the band played a slow song, he asked Barbara for a dance. She was swept off her feet by this young man whom she had always seen as aloof and quiet. By the end of the evening, Raj had told Barbara of the sorry state his marriage was in and how he craved company every evening. He told her that his wife had refused to move to New Delhi, choosing to stay in her hometown, and that she was averse to all physical contact with him.

Barbara, starry-eyed as she was about him, bought into his story.

'Oh Raj, I feel so bad for you. You have no one to look after you and you work so hard all the time,' she said.

'I know,' he replied. 'I am so lonely.'

While dropping her home, he gallantly got out of the car and went to the other side to open the door. As Barbara got out, she held his shoulder to balance herself. He kissed her gently. Barbara was expecting this and kissed him back.

'Let's go up to your apartment,' Raj whispered to her and she nodded.

They fell into each other's arms as the door of her apartment closed behind her. He tore open her blouse and pulled down her skirt.

'Please be gentle with me,' she whispered.

'Don't worry, my darling. Trust me,' he responded as he led her into the bedroom, kissing her passionately. They fell on her bed and made love. Raj spent the night with her and they made love three times.

What had started as a simple dinner date led to them seeing each other regularly at his or her apartment. They would wait for the evening and rush back, desperate to make love.

Barbara enjoyed Raj's touch and liked spending time with him. His education and his knowledge of world affairs impressed her greatly and she loved to hear him talk. All that she craved for was to feel his strong arms around her.

There would be days when Raj had to work late and would ask her to meet him in the executive toilet for a quick rendezvous. After he was done, he would leave the toilet and return to his office. He had no interest in her satisfaction. She would follow a few minutes later after cleaning up. They would continue working as if nothing had happened.

Barbara believed there was a future in this relationship and did everything to be available to Raj whenever he needed her. He, though, was very certain that he needed her only for his physical gratification. He definitely did not see any long-term relationship with Barbara or any woman other than his wife.

His dalliances with Barbara came to the attention of the HR director at a company party. Rumours were floating around in the company that Raj was seeing Barbara regularly. Several people had seen her going to his apartment on many evenings and she had been spotted on his balcony on weekends. Someone had seen both of them come out of the same toilet. The corporate world thrives on the company grapevine and Trust Corporation was no exception.

Relationships between employees were frowned upon in the company.

Rumour had it that Mrs D'Souza had been observing Raj and Barbara. She had never liked Raj from the minute she had first met him, when he had come for his interview.

'You should look at the relationship between Raj and his secretary,' she stated casually to the HR director's secretary one morning. 'They seem to be a little too friendly, and I have been seeing the lady in the executive toilet quite often.'

The HR director, on hearing this, picked up the signal

immediately. After some preliminary investigation, he asked Anita to have a chat with Raj about this matter.

That very morning, Anita walked into Raj's office and said, 'Raj, I have come to discuss a sensitive matter about you. It is awkward for me to discuss this but I have been asked to have a word with you. The company understands from reliable sources that you have been spending far too much time with your secretary. It would be advisable if you put an end to this matter quickly in your own interest and that of Trust. The company does not wish to be faced with any embarrassing situation later.'

Raj was a ruthless individual. Nothing mattered to him more than himself. He had always been very clear that he would never allow anything to compromise his interests.

This discussion came as a huge shock to him, because he had thought that he was being very discreet.

'What ridiculous allegations, Anita!' he said angrily. 'You know that I am happily married with two children. How can you accuse me of an affair?'

'Raj, I understand your position. As your friend, I was asked to communicate this message to you by the director. Remember, there is no smoke without fire. The rest is up to you,' she replied.

'You can transfer Barbara from my office immediately if you think there is anything between us,' Raj told Anita.

Anita decided not to push the matter any further. She always avoided confrontations with another colleague. She had Barbara transferred to the secretarial pool the next day.

Raj stopped seeing Barbara immediately, without giving any reasons to her. Barbara tried to contact him in the office and at his home several times, but he made himself completely inaccessible.

Within a week, Raj filed a complaint with the HR department that some money was missing from his office drawer. He suspected that his former secretary had stolen it.

HR did a quick enquiry and though they found no evidence, they took the word of a company manager over his secretary's and asked her to submit her resignation. Barbara tried her best to save her job, but as she could not disclose the relationship she'd had with Raj, she had no choice but to resign.

'Leave no telltale signs in any relationship,' Raj would tell himself afterwards. 'In future, only pay and play. Never get emotion involved.'

Not once did it cross his mind that his indiscretions were wrong. His belief was that as long as he was not falling in love with another woman and while he was providing well for his wife and children, what he was doing was okay.

He had no desire to be faithful to his wife or any other woman and went back to regular paid sex, though this time he was much more careful.

He had much greater ability to pay now as compared to his college days. Wherever he travelled, he was able to find a release for his physical needs. A lady was always available in his hotel room for a price, and some grateful hotel staff member who had been tipped well was always available to make arrangements. He vowed to himself that he would not get involved in any emotional relationship again.

Lovely knew of her husband's weakness. Though she suspected him several times when she unpacked his bags and found packets of condoms in his shaving kit, which she knew would never be used with her, she chose to keep quiet.

However, on one of her visits to Raj in New Delhi while he was having an affair with Barbara, she found clear signs of a woman in his house. She gathered up courage and asked him about the condoms in his bathroom drawer. He simply shrugged away her question saying, 'Don't you trust me?' She had no answer.

'These must have been lying there for a long time. After all, you and I have not slept together for so many years. Stop making a hill out of a mole,' he told Lovely.

~

Raj always believed that he was extremely discreet and that Lovely would never find out about his escapades. On the other hand, Lovely believed that as long as she and her children were financially looked after, there was no reason to complain. She felt that as long as she pretended not to know anything, she would be safe and happy.

Over the years, Lovely demanded lesser and lesser attention from Raj and built her world around her children. She stopped expecting anything from her husband, so if he did bring anything for her or spent time with her, she was pleasantly surprised. They both built separate lives for themselves. However, the thought of separating from her husband never crossed her mind; partly because she was not independent financially and partly because she believed that they should stay together for the sake of their children.

This arrangement also suited Raj since he wanted time to be on his own and yet liked to think of himself as the anchor of his family. With his wife and children settled in Chandigarh he felt that his familial duties had been done and plunged himself into the world of corporate politics and work.

When his father fell ill and needed a coronary bypass, Raj was unable to go for the surgery because he was busy with the company's annual plan presentations. The thought of being by his father's bedside did not cross his mind. However, he took comfort in the fact that Lovely would look after his father and nurse him back to health. He justified this lapse to himself, thinking, I have sent all the money that was needed for the surgery. Besides, have I not sacrificed my own comforts by leaving my wife with my parents so that she can look after them?

He convinced himself that he was a loving son who was doing what was expected of him.

~

Trust Corporation was making large investments in the power sector and given its strong cash flows from the alcohol business, these capital-intensive projects were largely funded by internal cash accruals. The large capital expenditures also provided significant depreciation benefits, which resulted in tax savings and hence even more free cash for the company.

Raj had a flexible conscience that he could mould to believe whatever he liked. He could quell his conscience easily during his various affairs. Similarly, his conscience kept changing as he rose within the hierarchy.

The corporate policy of Trust Corporation prohibited anyone from accepting any gifts, either in cash or kind, from any supplier or business associate. However, as a young manager, Raj did not stop a small supplier from sending him a box of sweets on Diwali. When in middle management, he did not return a carton of twelve bottles of Johnnie Walker Red Label whisky, which was sent by another supplier to secure an order.

Once, when he was sent a colour television, he called the supplier and said, 'Since I already have a colour television, can you take this back and send me cash instead?'

He had completely subdued his conscience.

~

Setting up power plants was a slow and expensive process, involving a lot of interaction with local politicians and bureaucrats. As a young manager, Raj was involved in a number of decisions being made by the company. He was often asked to pay small sums of money to various government bodies to speed up approvals needed to expedite the implementation of a project.

Trust Corporation was covered by stringent anti-corruption laws and the Indian top management was a signatory to the Foreign Corrupt Practices Act. However, the local management in their wisdom had decided that it was easier to cover up some expenditures and meet project deadlines rather than delay a project. Audit checks from the international headquarters used to take place regularly, but a smart finance director was able to conceal these payments by submitting relevant bills.

The management felt that as long as they 'did not know where the money was being given' they were conforming to the law. They handled these payments through company agents, who would raise consultancy bills on the company which would be paid promptly. The top management assumed that Raj would also follow the same practice and work only through an authorized agent when it came to the matter of making payments.

'We don't know and we don't care. As long as we don't know, we are okay' was their standard party line if they were ever quizzed about corruption. This was so ingrained within the organization that they would repeat the same lines at internal company parties and smile knowingly.

In order to get some approvals, Raj was asked to handle some payments by his senior manager. Young Raj was very excited the first time he held a huge sum of ₹50,000. This amount was several times larger than his monthly salary. While making the payment, he quietly took out two hundred-rupee notes from each bundle and handed over the balance to the contact. The middleman did not bother to count the money, since he had complete trust in the company; Raj became richer by ₹1,000 without doing any work.

'That was easy,' he thought to himself. That night, he gave an extra fifty rupees as tip to the young girl who had been brought to his room by the hotel doorman.

His sticky fingers started to get used to this easy money. He knew that taking a few notes out of every bundle of currency notes would never be found out, and in any case by the time the notes were finally counted, they would have passed through at least two, if not more hands. No one would be any the wiser on where the shortfall had occurred.

To meet his growing need for money to fulfill his lavish lifestyle, Raj started to look for other opportunities to make small sums of money.

When he was asked to lead a negotiation to procure land around the power project to build company housing, he convinced himself that there was nothing wrong in accepting a sum of one hundred thousand rupees from a local property broker and agreeing to a higher rate per square metre.

After all, as he rationalized to himself, 'I am getting a good deal for the company and this land will be worth a lot of money in the years to come. That is when everyone will thank me for my presight. Besides, this is a small percentage of the value of the land and they can never find out.'

Since he had not been caught the first time, he became bolder with each transaction and the amount of cash stashed away in the locker of his Godrej stainless steel cupboard at home kept growing.

He had never seen so much money before and since he had no one at home to ask him any questions, he started to spend this on expensive whisky, clothes and women. At the same time, he was conscious of the fact that he must not buy any assets about which his friends and colleagues could ask questions.

~

Raj never compromised on his work, and this quality was recognized by his seniors. He was a workaholic and made no bones about it. He was also known to insist that all his subordinates needed to stay in office as long as he was there, and he never went home before 7 p.m. Unlike other managers in the power division, he had no family and was able to spend long periods away from New Delhi at the site offices. He was never in a hurry to fly home for a birthday or an anniversary and was happy to base himself wherever required for extended periods of time to get work completed.

Over the next few years, recognizing his hard work, he was given two quick promotions in the company. His indiscretion with Barbara had been forgotten and his dipping into the company coffers had not been caught by anyone.

By the turn of the decade, Raj was one of the youngest deputy general managers and he knew there was no looking back.

~

Sangeeta

Sangeeta and Major Ajay Sharma had started their married life with both of them going their separate ways to New Delhi and Srinagar respectively. Ajay knew that this was not what he had wanted. However, once he had made the commitment to his wife, there was not much that he could do. He had tried very hard to get the army to give him approval to allow her to visit him in Kashmir, but the Government of India refused him permission each time he applied.

Sangeeta, on the other hand, was happy with this arrangement. She had wanted space in their marriage and she had got it. Realizing that she was lucky to have found such a cooperative husband, she resolved to do her bit to make the marriage work. Ajay was entitled to two months' annual leave every year and since she could not visit him, he would visit her in New Delhi as often as he could.

Though he wanted her to travel with him on vacations, she was seldom able to take any leave. The first time he visited her, they went out for a nice cozy dinner at The Oberoi Maidens Hotel in Civil Lines, Old Delhi. She made a booking at The Cavalry Bar for a drink, followed by dinner at The Curzon Room. Ajay had never visited such an expensive restaurant in his life and when he looked at the prices on the menu, he was shocked.

'Sangeeta, I think we should go somewhere else. I cannot afford this place,' he said.

'Don't worry about the money, Ajay. I earn enough for both of us and this will be my treat to you,' Sangeeta replied, not realizing that she could be offending his manly pride.

She ordered expensive white wine for herself and a large Scotch for him at The Cavalry Bar, where she thought he would be happy seeing so many old army artifacts. The food, too, was exquisite.

To a young army officer, who had grown up drinking Old Monk rum and eating tasteless food and watery caramel custard for dessert at the National Defence Academy and later at the various army officers' messes, this was an unimaginable treat.

The bill for the evening came to four hundred rupees, which was as much as Ajay made in one month. The fact that his wife had to pay for their first celebratory meal left him seething, but he pursed his lips, swallowed his pride and kept quiet.

~

The software business was beginning to take root in India, and between customer visits and overseas travel Sangeeta spent less and less time at home. By now, she had started to stay away from home for a couple of days every week. In the first few years, she would try and adjust her travels to stay in New Delhi when Ajay was visiting so that they could spend time together. But as her workload increased, she started to travel even when Ajay was in town. She would justify this by thinking that she was only going to be away for one or two nights.

Their first major argument was etched clearly in Sangeeta's mind for years to come.

In order to spend more time with Ajay, she had taken an

early morning flight at 6 a.m. from Delhi to Bombay, leaving home at 4 a.m. She returned the following day by the last flight, getting home at 11 p.m.

Ajay was fast asleep as she tiptoed into the house, tired and hungry. She changed quietly in the guest room, slipped into their bed and reached out to hold her husband. Ajay was awake, but angry with her. He turned over to face the opposite wall and pretended to be fast asleep.

The next morning he was quiet as they sat together for a cup of tea.

'You have been away for three days. I come here to spend time with you, but you never seem to have any time for me,' he said.

'How can that be?' she countered. 'I left home on Monday morning by the first flight and came back yesterday night by the last flight. So it is really one night that I was away. Can't you see how much I am pushing myself and how tiring such trips can be?'

He did not agree with her logic of the number of days she had been away. To him, she had been away for three nights.

'You slept early the night before you had to travel because of your early morning flight and yesterday you returned almost at midnight, by which time I was asleep,' Ajay responded. 'Which means you have been away for three nights, as far as I am concerned. As for getting tired, you take flights and you stay in five-star hotels. How can you be tired?'

Sangeeta did not agree with his argument, but sensed his anger and chose to remain quiet. She too was angry that he was not willing to understand her work commitments.

That evening, when she returned from work, Ajay was not at home. He returned late at night and when she asked him where he had been, he replied, 'With my batchmates from the National Defence Academy at the army officers' mess. You would not be interested in meeting them. They are not your corporate types.'

With that, he walked away angrily into their bedroom and went to sleep.

However, Ajay was back to normal the next morning and made conversation as if nothing had happened. Sangeeta had been irritated with his behaviour the previous night, but her only way of showing anger was to keep quiet. So she said nothing and went off to work without eating anything.

Seeing her cold reaction, Ajay too decided to keep quiet on the subject.

When she returned home, they said nothing to each other and after dinner, went to sleep in separate bedrooms.

Their first cold war lasted twenty-four hours. They forced themselves to start talking again the next day because Ajay's annual leave was coming to an end.

~

As time passed and Sangeeta's travels increased, she tried to keep in touch with Ajay over the phone but getting through to him was a big challenge. STD calls from New Delhi to Srinagar were difficult to connect and even when she did manage to get through, the cost was ₹42 per minute, which, even on her private sector salary, was expensive.

When she could not get through on STD, she would book a trunk call. There would be times when she would wait for an entire day to get a call through to him. When she did manage to get through, she would be at the mercy of the trunk call operator who, after every three minutes, would say that the time was up.

'Please extend it,' she would request.

'Hurry up and finish, madam. Many people waiting in the queue,' the operator would respond.

After giving them a maximum of nine minutes, the trunk operator would unilaterally decide to disconnect the phone. This was a common problem in India in the 1980s, with business and personal conversations being governed by uncaring and unconcerned phone operators.

Ajay would also try calling through his army exchange, but it was only good for internal defence communications, impossible for other calls. He would sometimes try and call from the STD/ISD booth in the local market, but the costs were prohibitive for him. Calling Sangeeta when she was travelling overseas was even more expensive, and he had to think several times before doing so.

The lack of communication between Ajay and Sangeeta started to increase. They began to feel that there was not much to say to the other over phone, since they were not involved in each other's daily lives. Letters took a long time to reach and neither was able to sustain letter writing for an extended period of time.

Between her travel, lack of communication with Ajay and no one to come back to at home, Sangeeta started to spend longer hours at work.

She used to change her travel schedule when she was trying to spend more time with Ajay. Now she did not care, and in order to rest she started taking an evening flight and returning two days later by a morning flight, thus spending three nights away from home for a two-day trip. But with so much travelling, despite two extra nights in hotels, she would always feel tired.

Sangeeta's overseas trips would last at least ten days and when she returned home she would be jet-lagged and needing sleep.

Meanwhile, Ajay was transferred in quick succession to Lucknow and Ahmedabad. Upon each transfer he would pack his bags himself. He requested the government to give him a posting in New Delhi on compassionate grounds but this was denied to him.

He would watch his colleagues move and see how couples with their young children would pack their belongings in wooden and metal boxes. He had to do everything on his own and since he had never really set up a proper home, he had very limited belongings.

Sangeeta was never able to find the time to be with him when he moved home or to help him set up his home in the new city. On his part, Ajay continued to visit her at least for two weeks every quarter, knowing full well that he was trying extra hard to save their marriage, and unsure if his wife was making a similar effort.

Every evening that Sangeeta came home late from work, he would complain and go into a sulk. She would try to explain the reasons but he remained unconvinced. His sulking would lead to days of no communication. They would eat dinner and sleep in the same bed without exchanging a word. She would leave for office the next morning without anything being said between them.

Both Sangeeta and Ajay realized that their differences were increasing. They mutually understood that they should not complicate their marriage further by having children. Without children to anchor their marriage and virtually no interest in each other's lives, they started doing things on their own. Ajay's visits to New Delhi also started to reduce after the first five years of marriage.

Given their differences, Ajay refused to conform to the social requirements of Trust Corporation and more often than not, would excuse himself from attending company functions.

'Why do you expect me to comply with your company's requirements when you will not conform to mine?' he would say.

'You are visiting me in New Delhi, which is why I want you to come with me to my company parties. When I come to your house, I will definitely come for your fauji parties,' Sangeeta would retort angrily.

'Why is it always your house and my house?' he would reply sharply. 'Why don't you ever say our home?'

'I promise I will come to your parties when I come to visit you,' Sangeeta would say in all sincerity.

'That will be the day!' he would respond sarcastically and walk off, only to start another cold war between them.

Sangeeta would try to justify his absence at parties to her colleagues. She was obsessed with her career and not willing to make any compromises on the work front. She was convinced that Ajay had no interest in her life. Their arguments and communication gap started to worsen until one morning, seven years later, Major Ajay Sharma walked out of her life, never to come back again, and filed for a divorce.

Sangeeta felt a huge weight lift off her shoulders. She had been living a charade. As she looked back at her seven years with Ajay, she recognized that her marriage had been doomed from the start. She made no effort at making any reconciliatory moves and signed the divorce papers immediately after she had received them.

Ajay and Sangeeta lived separately for twelve months while

waiting for the court to approve their divorce. The formal divorce came through a year later and the bitterness between them was so intense that they chose never to communicate again.

With nobody and nothing to come back to every evening, Sangeeta immersed herself in work with a vengeance. She pushed herself very hard and became an extremely demanding, sometimes unreasonable boss. Working late and working on weekends became the norm rather than the exception for her.

She had set out with the objective of running the company and she was determined that she would get there.

She had a point to prove to herself.

~

The software business was new for Trust Corporation. It was looking for a strong source to earn valuable foreign exchange for India. Most Indian companies were beginning to export commodities and agricultural products, generally at a loss, which was made up for by subsidies from the Government of India.

Trust Corporation was not in a position to export alcohol, since it was constrained from doing business outside Indian shores by its principal shareholder. In order to take attention away from its alcohol business, the company had entered the power and the software sectors.

There was general scepticism in the company about the prospects of the software business, given the fact that most senior managers were not comfortable using computers and viewed the newly installed machines in their offices as faster typing and word processing units through which their secretaries could print out nicely formatted letters.

The chairman had asked his vice-chairman to oversee the activities of the software business. This was done to ensure support for the business across the company, so that it would not stumble before it got going because of a lack of understanding of its potential by various managers.

The business of the new decade needed managers with a new perspective. The managers in the HR department had been asked to find 'an outgoing person with a pleasant personality who may have networks in international companies' for the software division.

Sangeeta had been posted to the software division primarily because she fitted this job description very well. She was aggressive, outgoing, had a pleasing personality and had been educated at Harvard Business School. Her US citizenship enabled her to travel to various countries without applying for a visa, which was needed for managers with Indian passports.

Like all young and upcoming software companies, Trust Corporation had also started their operations with 'body shopping'. Salary levels in India were significantly lower than the salary levels in USA for comparable jobs. These software companies were essentially taking advantage of an arbitrage opportunity in the salary differential between Indian and international salaries. They would hire young engineers from good colleges and send them overseas. The fact that a large number of these youngsters chose not to come back did not bother these companies too much, because there was a large supply of trained manpower in India. The software 'expert' would be sent on a significantly higher salary as compared to what he was earning in India, yet the company would earn three times his salary from their customer.

Trust Corporation India had the added advantage of a US parent, so the first few people from India were 'exported' to the parent company. While the parent company got the advantage of getting employees at lower salaries, the Indian company was able to use the first contract as a reference for making marketing calls to other international clients.

Sangeeta was required to travel quite extensively to Europe and USA during this time and given her deteriorating relationship with her husband, she actually started to enjoy being away for long periods.

Her boss was not aware of the exact problems in her marriage but sensed that there was something amiss. He knew that Sangeeta and Ajay lived in separate cities because of their respective careers. He had noticed that they never attended a single company party together. Sangeeta always came alone. She never called home during the day and she was never in a hurry to go home. He often counselled her to spend more time at home and tried to send her away early on long weekends when he knew that her husband was in town.

Sangeeta would never admit that her marriage was on the rocks to anyone, including herself.

She brushed away her boss's advice, lying, 'Sir, my husband understands and appreciates my work. He is very supportive of my career.'

Her boss did not push any further. He did not want to interfere in the life of a junior colleague. Besides, why would he mind? She was an excellent worker and willing to take on additional responsibilities. Besides, she never shirked from working long hours at the office. She would also not complain if she was asked to travel at short notice within or outside India. Her bags were always packed and ready. Her personal life was hers to resolve.

The software business had a slow but sure start. The advantage of this venture was that large investments did not need to be made in infrastructure and all the margins that were made flowed through directly to the bottom line of the company. In addition to the profits of the division, the company also gained large tax savings because of export incentives that were given by the government.

Sangeeta was promoted regularly every few years and by the time she had finished ten years with Trust Corporation, she had reached the rank of deputy general manager in the software division.

~

Iqbal

Iqbal and Samina moved to New Delhi soon after their marriage. They shifted into their company-allotted apartment and Samina efficiently took charge of running their home. Married life was not very exciting for them; they quickly settled into a routine. They were both very conservative in making love and Iqbal was always the initiator. Samina had been taught that ladies must never make the first move. Their union was always hurried, with the primary purpose of producing children.

Iqbal had been very pampered by his mother when he was young and soon after that he had been sent off to study at a boarding school. Since he had never learned to do anything on his own at home, he was very comfortable in letting Samina take the lead in managing their house. He was not prepared to do any work or share in household duties. He firmly believed that the man must not interfere at home and the lady must not interfere outside.

'I have never done any housework,' he once told his wife proudly. Samina had been told the same by his mother soon after their marriage, and though she did not agree with it, she decided not to comment.

She would do all the household chores through the morning, sleep in the afternoon and then wait for Iqbal to return from work. She would serve him a fried snack with his evening tea after which they would have an early dinner.

Iqbal did not drink, so once he was home there was not much to do except watch television. They would watch *Chitrahaar* every Wednesday and the Sunday movie on Doordarshan. Iqbal would watch the 8 p.m. and 9 p.m. news without fail, though there would be virtually no change in the content. Generally, they would then turn in early, only to start the same routine the following morning.

Weekends were for sleeping late for him, while she cooked and finished all the work at home before he woke up. If Iqbal was in a good mood, he would take Samina shopping at the local market on his Bajaj Chetak scooter, a gift he had received from Samina's parents at their wedding. If he was tired or grumpy, she would walk across the street to the local kirana shop and buy provisions for the week ahead. She would never ask him for anything and meekly accepted his bidding all the time.

Iqbal had never forgotten his homosexual experience in school. Every time he thought of it, he would get very angry with himself. He coupled his guilt at his lapse with anger at the financial letdown by his older brothers. He blamed them for his having to work for a living.

Iqbal had always had a very short temper and he started to vent his anger against Samina at the slightest excuse.

'Why are you blaming me?' she would often ask him when he was upset.

'I am not blaming you, but you represent my family's choice because they selected you to marry me,' he would retort in irrational anger.

Coming from a traditional family, she accepted his bouts of anger silently, hoping that he would change someday.

She would pack his lunch every morning, taking care not to repeat the menu more than once a week, as otherwise she would be taunted in the evening about the lack of variety in her cooking. She once made the mistake of reacting to this.

'You should be glad you have a person who cooks a meal for you,' she replied and immediately knew she had made a big mistake.

The sharp slap across her face left the red mark of Iqbal's fingers on her cheek. She did not know how to react. Her husband had just slapped her. As she cringed to avoid another slap and covered her face, tears welling in her eyes from the hurt and the shock, he screamed at her, 'Never, ever answer me back in this tone or question me in future! You are my wife and I expect you to do what I tell you.'

Samina said nothing, just sobbed quietly.

Iqbal felt no regret about slapping her. On the contrary, he experienced a strong sense of control as he saw her shrink away, tears in her eyes, a shocked look on her face. This was one aspect of his personality she had never seen. His face was red and his hands were shaking in anger. His heartbeat had increased significantly, his muscles had tensed and his breathing had become sharp and fast.

Suddenly, Iqbal felt the muscles inside his neck and throat tighten. He tried to take a deep breath, but felt a constriction in his throat and lungs. The shortness of breath left him gasping for air. He sat down on a chair holding the armrest and tried to take deep breaths.

'I cannot breathe,' he said hoarsely.

Despite the shock of the slap, Samina realized that something was wrong and ran to the kitchen to get him a glass of water. When the breathing did not normalize, she called a neighbour.

They rushed him to a hospital where he was put on oxygen. This helped him to start breathing normally again.

The intense anger against Samina had triggered an asthma attack in Iqbal. He had been mildly asthmatic as a child but had never felt any serious trouble in breathing till now.

When he felt better and came home, he blamed Samina for the asthma attack: 'You made me angry. If you had kept quiet, I would not have fallen sick.'

Samina bowed her head in submission, not wanting to provoke his anger and risk another slap.

~

Iqbal was eligible for membership of two of the premier clubs of the city as per company policy. Though he took the membership and kept it throughout his career, he never took advantage of any of the clubs' facilities.

He visited them a few times when he had first joined the company, and quickly concluded that these were watering holes for people to drink and socialize. Since he did not touch alcohol, he did not see any additional value in frequenting the clubs. He did not use the extensive sports facilities provided by them either, as he did not believe in exercising.

'What a waste of time and money,' he told his co-workers and stopped going altogether.

Iqbal was very careful with his money, given the loss of his family's fortunes, and controlled his monthly salary himself. He would give Samina money to buy household provisions and would always ask for detailed accounts of every rupee spent by her. Only when he was convinced that she had spent the money carefully and correctly would he agree to give her more.

She got used to the question, '*Batao paise kahan kharch kiye?*

Where have you spent the money?' She would make detailed notes of the expenditure and give these to him for approval.

Iqbal did not introduce Samina to the club life. She too did not know any better and was happy with what she had. They did not socialize much as a couple and chose to make a small group of friends from within their community, spending all their time together in one another's homes. The primary focus of such social gatherings was food. Each lady tried to outdo the others in the meal to be served in her home.

The only exception Iqbal made to his rule of 'no partying' was when he was invited to a large office party hosted by the finance department of his company. However, he chose to go alone, preferring to keep Samina away from his colleagues.

Within a few months of their marriage, Samina got pregnant and delivered a baby boy. Iqbal was present in the hospital for the delivery. When he received the news of his son, he knelt on the hospital floor to offer thanks to God for giving him a healthy heir. He distributed sweets to all the hospital staff and took a box of sweets next morning to his office as well.

When Samina and their son came home, Iqbal returned to his normal life at work and his usual behaviour at home, though he was careful about raising his voice too much at Samina. She was, after all, the mother of his child.

However, he had not been prepared for the arrival of the baby. He was not willing to commit so much of his time and energy to his child. He was selfish and wanted time to himself. He moved out of their bedroom into the guest bedroom so that his sleep would not be disturbed. He left the upbringing of their son entirely to Samina.

'I need my sleep, Samina. After all, I work so hard every day in the office. Besides, looking after the child is your responsibility,' he would say if Samina ever gave him a sign that she was tired.

Samina delivered two more sons in quick succession in the next two years. In three years Iqbal and Samina's family had grown from two members to five, and Iqbal could sense a strain on his personal finances.

'How will we manage our expenses? You need to be very careful, Samina,' he would tell her often.

Samina had to now manage three young children, as well do all the washing, cooking and cleaning. As always, Iqbal chose not to help her at all. He did relent later and hired a maid after the third boy, when he saw that she was not being able to handle all three crying children at night and found his own sleep being disturbed.

'Children are to be seen and not heard' was his belief and he adhered to it when it came to his children.

After their third son, Iqbal stopped reaching out to Samina at night. He did not want any more children and since this was the only purpose of their making love, he decided it was better to stop his nocturnal dalliances with his wife completely, rather than risk another baby.

Their sons started school and other than paying their school fees, Iqbal was never interested in their progress. If he was ever asked the name of the school, he would need a minute to think before responding. He was never able to correctly state the class his children were in and he had no knowledge of their performance in academics. Samina signed all the monthly school reports and attended all parent-teacher meetings alone.

The three boys were very scared of their father. Partly due to fear and partly because of regular cautioning from their mother, they had learned to stay out of his way at home. They would leave for school before he woke up. By the time he came home, they would be playing downstairs. When he went for his shower and evening prayers, Samina gave them dinner and packed them off to their bedroom to watch television.

'Papa's coming' was enough to scare the boys and send them scurrying off to their room.

Iqbal seldom remembered his sons' birthdays, and while they expected birthday greetings from him in their early years, as they grew older they stopped noticing whether or not their father had wished them. Iqbal did not miss talking to his sons every day either, nor did he want to be a part of their lives. He did not miss their warm bodies as they cuddled up to their mother because he had chosen to sleep in a separate bedroom. His bedroom was almost out of bounds for his three sons.

The boys, who were barely a year apart from each other in age and very closely bonded, learned to keep themselves occupied and happy. Their lives revolved around their mother, who had all the time in the world for her sons, and they worshipped her.

Their father was no longer a part of their lives and they did not miss him at all.

~

Iqbal was very ambitious and deep inside, he continued to stoke his fire of resentment against his brothers and his family to keep himself motivated. Had it not been for their throwing away the family fortunes, his life would have been very different.

He exhibited his sharp tongue and short temper with the people working for him too, though he was very careful with about he spoke and behaved with his superiors.

Though he did not drink alcohol or smoke cigarettes, he

enjoyed chewing gutka. His waste-paper basket in the office and his washbasin at home bore telltale signs of his addiction. Consuming tobacco was not good for his asthma, but Iqbal was unable to give it up. He started taking regular medication for his asthma but continued to eat more and stronger gutka every day.

His office life was a routine of working with the chief accountant to ensure that accounts and trial balances were drawn up in time, reports were sent to the board members as per schedule and financial feedback to the various stakeholders of the company was always true and fair.

~

Trust Corporation had always treated its finance managers with a lot of respect. All young managers were trained to blow the whistle anytime they sensed a problem. This cautious approach had helped the company build strong systems and processes in a complex environment.

The finance managers were the 'watchdogs' of the company and the finance director, India, reported to the finance director in USA. The company also had an all-powerful internal audit department whose managers were permitted to go into any office, unannounced, and conduct an audit. Their itinerary was known only to the general manager (audit), who reported to the finance director. Iqbal spent the first year in the internal audit department, which gave him a good understanding of the three businesses and the key managers in each business.

He liked the power he derived as a member of the internal audit department.

Iqbal had a sharp mind for numbers and he made himself extremely valuable within the department in a short period. He could compute numbers in his mind faster than most people, and was nicknamed 'Calculator' by his colleagues.

He would study the monthly divisional reports very carefully to understand what was happening within the organization and prepared intelligent comparative analyses of the various businesses. He presented these numbers graphically on chart papers within his department.

The finance director liked this young man who always came prepared for all meetings and unfailingly had the right answer to his questions. Iqbal was also particularly careful to complete any work given by the finance director before he returned home at night, so that when the boss came into work the next morning, the assignment would already be on the finance director's table.

He was fortunate that he was sometimes asked to accompany his boss to the board meetings, even though he sat unnoticed in a corner of the boardroom while the all-powerful board of Trust Corporation deliberated and discussed the plans and strategy for each of their three business groups. This exposure to high-level strategic sessions was invaluable for the young man at this early stage of his career, and not many people could have asked for more.

If, during a meeting, the finance director turned around and asked him for any extra information, Iqbal's chest would swell with pride. While his other management trainee batchmates were sweating it out in the field, working in various divisions, he was fortunate to be sitting in an air-conditioned office and interacting with the top management.

Information was power for Iqbal. He would give out small snippets of news from the board meeting to fuel the corporate grapevine, though he was careful not to disclose too much, which could have got him into trouble.

Iqbal also loved to keep his eyes and ears open to hear any gossip or rumours about his colleagues. He never knew when he could use this information to turn the tide against a colleague. He would look through all expense claim vouchers to see where his colleagues had travelled and whether there were any unusual expenses. He would ask the clerks in the finance department about the khabar in other departments. He would go to work on some Saturdays and Sundays to see who was working and who was misusing company facilities. It was not unusual for him to rummage through his colleagues' waste-paper baskets to find any interesting information. He would examine residential and office telephone bills so that he could track managers making personal calls.

Iqbal also used his proximity to the finance director to give the director information from the informal grapevine of the company. He would casually talk about individual managers and their dalliances, as well as give details about any invoices that may have been irregularly processed by other managers.

He became a source of power for the finance director, who loved to hear this kind of gossip.

Iqbal also used this little power he had to run down Rahul, Raj, Anita and Sangeeta, as well as other senior colleagues and superiors, whenever he could.

'Sir, I understand that Raj is having an affair with his secretary,' he would say. Or, 'Sir, I have heard from reliable sources that Sangeeta and her husband are heading for a separation.' Or, 'Sir, have you met Anita's husband Michael? Quite a good-for-nothing fellow.' Or, 'Sir, Rahul is travelling too much. You should start a check on all his expense claims.' Or, 'Sir, the STD calls being made from the HR department are unusually high. It looks like personal calls are being made by Anita. I can have this investigated if you want me to.'

Fortunately for the company, the finance director was a man of strong convictions and though he loved to hear all this, he seldom took any action unless he had verified the veracity of the news himself.

However, he did not stop Iqbal from sharing these rumours. He was never sure when he could pick up a nugget of information that would help him further his own career as the next vice-chairman of the company.

By the end of the eighties, after having spent ten years with the company, Iqbal was promoted to the rank of deputy general manager in the finance department. No one could grudge him the promotion, which he had earned through sheer hard work and determination to succeed.

Most of his peers and superiors within the finance function started to feel insecure because of his sharp mind and frequent promotions.

~

Anita

Michael and Anita settled easily into their two-bedroom company apartment in New Delhi with their few belongings

Michael had brought his Royal Enfield motorcycle as well, and the two of them would love to go racing down the streets of New Delhi. Anita would hold him round his waist, her hair open and flying as he revved up his motorcycle on the open roads.

They would go out to restaurants and coffee shops in the city, and the fact that Michael never paid for anything never crossed her mind. She was excited and content to have him all to herself.

Michael had never been a doer, but he knew how to treat and satisfy his woman, and Anita did not have any complaints on this score.

After years of trying his hand at several small businesses and a few jobs, none of which had worked out, Michael was happy to have a permanent roof over his head. Coupled with this was the even stronger assurance that his wife was earning well and would make sure that he always had money in his pocket.

Michael decided that this comfortable life was what he had been looking for. He would wake up late, go for lunch to the Gymkhana Club, flirt with the club receptionist and the other staff members, drink his customary 'two double vodka tonics', come home to sleep in the afternoon and then wait for Anita to return in the evening and cook his dinner.

He had always been a fitness enthusiast and on Anita's pushing, he started to work out in the club gym and play squash on selected days of the week.

Anita's sense of victory after she married Michael was beginning to dull. Life was not a bed of roses. She was too meek to push her husband into working and though she often thought of asking him to do some work, she was never able to muster the courage to do so, because of the fear that she might lose him.

Michael understood her insecurity and used it effectively to manage her whenever he thought she was likely to push him or ask him why he did not take up a job or why his club bills were so high.

'You seem to have spent a lot of time at the club last month,' Anita would say, wondering how she would pay all his bills.

'Well, what else do you expect from me? I have to remain fit for you. Surely you will not grudge your husband a few drinks,' he would respond. She would bite her lips and keep quiet.

Each time he sensed that she was going to ask him to take up a job he would go away from New Delhi for a few days without telling her, leaving her in a complete state of panic, wondering if he had walked out on her. When he would return after several days, it was always to an adoring wife.

'Where were you in the last few days? I have been so worried,' Anita would exclaim.

'I thought I would take a break. After all, you never have time for me,' Michael would reply in a matter-of-fact tone.

She knew that he was blackmailing her and taking advantage

of her insecurity, but there was nothing she could do about it.

She started her work in earnest in the HR department. Though she was generally a soft-spoken person, she was also ambitious and keen to prove to herself that she could rise to the very top of the organization. The company had never promoted anyone from her function to the level of vice-chairman, and she hoped to be the first person to break the glass ceiling and make it to the corner office.

~

Anita was always worried about how Michael would react if she became pregnant. When she did conceive a baby, she waited for three months before mustering up the courage to tell him. She was pleasantly surprised to see his reaction.

'I am so excited, my dearest,' he told her. 'I will look after our child.'

Though he did not work, he led a lonely life. He told Anita that he would be the best father a baby could ever hope for. He would be there for their child every waking moment.

'This will relieve you of pressure at home, so that your work will not suffer,' he said.

When a baby daughter arrived, Michael, true to his word, took over all the responsibilities. He would wake up at night to feed and clean his daughter. He would be up early in the morning with the baby and take her out for long walks down the beautiful botanical gardens on Lodhi Road.

Their daughter had given him a purpose in life, and he soon stopped going for his daily vodka tonic and lunch to the club.

Anita was surprised at the change she saw in him, and with Michael taking charge of bringing up their baby, she was able to focus her energies on work.

~

The work in the HR department was very demanding, and Anita was soon immersed in it.

She started out by understanding the company's policies and was happy to see how employee-sensitive they were.

Trust Corporation was a compassionate organization and always believed in giving the benefit of doubt to an employee, unless it was a case of financial irregularities.

Issues relating to harassment at work had not yet surfaced or become serious problems in India in the 1980s.

Anita spent time in the payroll department, learned about all the statutory compliances that were required to be met every month and was involved in manpower planning. Since the company had a large presence in manufacturing, she was also given exposure to the nation's policies on industrial relations and the company's stand on such matters. Trust Corporation generally made sure that its policies were significantly better than the minimum expected by the Government of India.

She started to especially enjoy the work in the January to March quarter every year. This time period was generally referred to within the company as the HR quarter. This was the quarter when all appraisals were conducted and sent to the corporate office. This was also the period when promotions and increments were decided. Everyone's eyes were focused on the department for the annual promotions circular that was issued every year on 1 April.

People from across the country would call Anita in the second half of March to get a whiff of what might be happening in the HR department. Her friends and batchmates, Rahul, Raj, Sangeeta and Iqbal would suddenly discover her in March every year. They would all be keen to catch up with her for lunch, hoping that she would give them a hint whether any of their names was on the list of promotions.

'*Kya khabar*, Anita? What's the latest?' Iqbal would ask her as they bumped into each other in the corridors.

'Wait and watch,' she would respond coyly.

'I heard that the promotions list is very long this year,' Raj would say, hoping to get some signal.

'You know I cannot say anything, Raj,' she would reply.

Anita maintained the secrecy expected of her, though this knowledge did provide her a momentary source of power over her friends. The fact that she knew who would be promoted before anyone else made her feel important.

The company was always rife with rumours about forthcoming promotions and possible new organizational structures in each division. It was believed that if one looked at the hundreds of organizational structures drawn over lunch gossip, it was possible to form a fairly accurate assessment of what would finally come out on the due date.

The second quarter of the calendar year, April to June, which was also the first quarter of the new financial year, was when HR managers were busy handling resignations of people who had not been given the promotion or increment they had expected.

Anita started to work directly with the general manager, human resources, who in turn reported to the director, human resources. She would often find herself with the director, explaining why her department had made some recommendations. The exposure she got gave her a lot of self-confidence.

During an industrial dispute in one of the alcohol production units, Anita was sent as the representative from the head office. She had been trained in industrial relations at her management school and she worked along with the personnel manager of the factory to start negotiations with the factory union. In a few weeks, she managed to bring the union to a common set of objectives for the workers and the company and she, along with the factory manager, signed the settlement.

She received a note of appreciation from the vice-chairman 'for a job well done'.

By the turn of the decade, Anita had been promoted to senior manager. Though she was behind her batchmates by one level, her work was beginning to get recognition within the company and she was content with the progress being made in her career.

The Second Decade

The decade was changing again and everyone was looking forward to the 1990s, the last decade of the twentieth century, with hope and expectation.

Momentous events were taking place in the world.

Nelson Mandela had been freed after more than twenty-seven years in captivity. Iraq invaded Kuwait, setting off the Persian Gulf War. The Western Alliance ended the Cold War and proposed joint action with the Soviet Union. East and West Germany were united.

India had been managed by a series of coalition governments, which had brought the country to its knees. Prime Minister V. P. Singh's announcement on the implementation of the Mandal Commission led to a lot of agitation by the youth. Trade deficit was at record levels, foreign exchange reserves were at an all-time low and Prime Minister Chandra Shekhar had been forced to mortgage sixty-seven tonnes of gold with the World Bank, a move that was widely criticized since Indians believe that gold must never be mortgaged or sold.

Rajiv Gandhi was assassinated at Sriperumbudur on 21 May 1991 and soon after, P. V. Narasimha Rao was elected the prime minister of India. Rao brought in a strong team of ministers, including Manmohan Singh as the finance minister and P. Chidambaram as the commerce minister.

The new government had inherited an economy in shambles, as a result of several populist and expensive decisions taken by various governments in the eighties. With India's foreign exchange reserves at $1.2 billion in January 1991 and further depleted by half by June, barely enough to last for roughly three weeks of essential imports, the country was only weeks way from defaulting on its external balance of payment obligations.

The new finance minister, supported by the new prime minister, took quick and decisive steps to unshackle the 'caged tiger' and start the stalled process of liberalization. The steps taken by him breathed new life into the Indian economy and business houses responded very positively to this move. The Government of India constituted the Company Law Board as an independent quasi-judicial body, thus giving up direct control on matters of company law. Thousands of jobs were created as new businesses were started.

In the process of privatizing the public sector, the government opened up the archaic telecom sector and invited investments in infrastructure projects. Import tariffs were rationalized and imports were welcomed, instead of being seen as a drain on foreign exchange reserves.

~

Trust Corporation, after nearly eighty-five years of existence in India, was also looking at the new decade with ambitious investment plans. A liberalized and more open India would mean greater opportunities for them to reach out to their younger consumers.

The company had already committed large sums of money to their power business. When the new government announced its intention to open up the power sector further, as well as to consider privatization of power distribution, the organization discussed the possibilities of doubling their power generation capacity.

The alcohol business was robust as ever and continued to grow rapidly while generating huge cash surpluses, though senior management continued to downplay this business, given the social stigma attached to the product. More than 89 per cent of adults in India abstained from alcohol and more than 98 per cent of the women in India didn't drink. It was this large base of 'abstainers' that Trust Corporation saw as its potential market.

The software business had grown out of its infancy and Indian companies were making a mark on the international arena, though most of the software exports from India continued to be classified as 'body shopping'. Not many companies were considering developing indigenous products for the markets, since body shopping offered excellent returns with little investments. Trust Corporation was also sending a lot of workers to various clients in different countries and generating healthy cash surpluses.

~

There was a change of leadership at the top of Trust Corporation at the turn of the decade.

The chairman retired when he turned fifty-eight and the vice-chairman, who had been groomed for the past decade, stepped into his shoes. He was, like all past chairmen, a person who had started out as a management trainee in his early twenties. He knew the culture of the company like the back of his hand and no one expected anything new or different to happen during his tenure.

However, like all previous transitions, everyone expected a fallout in the board of directors, since only one of them could be anointed the next vice-chairman. This person would be selected by the new chairman in consultation with the shareholders, and would be the natural successor to the current chairman, barring any fiduciary irregularity. This practice of selecting the vice-chairman in advance was well entrenched so that the chairman could mentor the vice-chairman for the top job.

The new vice-chairman had been selected.

This time, unlike the previous vice-chairmen who were all from the alcohol division, the person selected was the finance director of the company. The message sent out was that the best man would be selected as the Number 2 person; there was no guarantee to the position simply because of time spent in the most profitable division.

With the top two managers in place, the shakeout started in the board of directors. The director of the alcohol division was the first to resign and take up a job with a competing company in the same business. Rahul was offered a position in the new company his mentor had moved to, but he declined gracefully.

'Thank you sir, but I would prefer to stay back and learn more. Once I am ready, I will definitely contact you,' he said, keeping his options open.

The next person to leave was the director of the power division. With so many power projects being set up in the country, it was not difficult for him to get a job as the CEO of another company offering significantly higher compensation.

Finally, the director of human resources also submitted his resignation. Though he had never been in the running, he too had hoped to be selected as the next vice-chairman.

'When giant trees fall, smaller plants get crushed as well'

is an old saying in the corporate world. It was no different in Trust Corporation.

Along with these top-level resignations, a number of senior and middle managers also went out of the system because they chose to follow their mentors into the new companies.

Transition at the top was seen as a healthy sign and not as a loss of good management staff. The churn in the top management also gave an opportunity for younger managers to rise faster up the ladder and revitalize the company structures with youth, energy and new ideas.

~

Rahul, Raj, Sangeeta, Iqbal and Anita were watching this transition of their top leadership very closely. They were also starting to understand how equations and power centres change so fast.

'Wow, I had never thought we would see three directors resign in such a short span of time,' said Anita.

'Well, this is good for all of us, isn't it? We get faster growth opportunities,' commented Raj.

'I am in good shape, since my boss is the new vice-chairman,' gloated Iqbal, 'but it looks like Rahul will have to start rebuilding his equations. All your hard work has been wasted.'

Rahul chose not to respond to Iqbal's barb.

Someday in the future, they, too, would be faced with similar choices and similar opportunities. They had learned a lot in the first ten years with Trust Corporation and were now moving into the middle and senior management. As colleagues, their paths had crossed very often in joint meetings and company off-sites and there was a lot of bonhomie amongst all five of them. They shared a common link because of their selection process.

All of them were aware that the 1990s would be the decade where they would start to compete more aggressively. This would also be a period when the better performers out of them would start to pull ahead of the pack. Each one was determined to lead. They had all been noticed and recognized by the senior management, but to get ahead from now onwards, they had to do something different at work.

Sangeeta, Rahul and Raj first came face-to-face with one another on a common platform in a company conference, where they were asked to lead discussion groups for their respective business groups. All three of them worked hard on their presentations and made their pitch to the top brass with a lot of passion and commitment.

'The alcohol business offers a sustained cash flow and large profits for our company,' said Rahul at the end of his presentation. 'We will be able to continue this growth well into the next decade, through innovation and category expansion.'

'The power business is new and is the right entry into the infrastructure space for us,' concluded Raj. 'I foresee a huge shortfall of power in our country in the next few decades and I believe that we should step in to bridge this gap.'

'The software business, unlike alcohol and power, is a sunrise business for our company and our country,' said Sangeeta. 'We have no investments, unlike our power business and we have no sensitivity issues, unlike our alcohol business. Our gross margins flow straight through to the bottom line.'

Sangeeta had been the most direct of the three, comparing her business with the other two.

The new chairman and vice-chairman, hearing their presentations, looked at each other. There was a ten-year age gap between the two of them and they worked well as a team, the chairman mentoring the vice-chairman. Both of them had been through a similar race in the first ten years of their tenure with Trust Corporation.

Their peers had fallen by the wayside and only the winners had survived. This rivalry and sense of competition was what would make the three youngsters run fast and hard. Eventually, the best person would be eligible for a shot at the top spot. They could see the healthy rivalry between the three young managers and they liked what they saw.

The company always encouraged teamwork, but when it came to leadership positions, they wanted to see individual initiative.

Sitting in the audience were Iqbal and Anita, listening to the presentations with rapt attention.

Iqbal was seated behind the vice-chairman. He had not been asked to make any presentation. Looking at the financial numbers in each presentation, he kept picking up the glaring errors that only a sharp finance mind like his could. He kept telling himself, 'I am sure I could have made these numbers come alive had I presented them. I would have shown the top management how every division hides their numbers.'

He had done a detailed analysis of each business and knew that he could tear into every presentation and show the bosses how the numbers were being misrepresented. For the moment, though, he had to satisfy himself by passing his comments on small pieces of paper to the vice-chairman.

Anita sat with a satisfied look, listening to all the discussions very carefully. She had not been asked to make any presentation either, but she was confident that her time to make a mark in front of the company's leadership would come in due course.

Both were wondering when they would get an opportunity

to speak to an audience as large as this and make their presence felt as well.

But they were in the back-office functions of the company; they would have to wait for a while before getting a similar opportunity.

~

That same evening, the chairman hosted a large party to celebrate the 'passing of the baton' to the new leadership, as well as to applaud the performance of the company and mark the start of the new decade.

Anita, Sangeeta, Raj, Rahul and Iqbal were invited to the party. They took this opportunity to network with senior managers who they normally would not have had a chance to meet.

Rahul was called by the chairman with a wave of his hand. This did not go unnoticed across the room.

'That was an excellent presentation, young man,' said the chairman. 'I am happy to see a fresh new perspective on our alcohol business, which continues to be our mainstay.'

'Thank you sir. I will do my best,' replied Rahul.

Raj managed to stand next to the vice-chairman. When asked what he thought of the alcohol presentation, he commented, 'It was good, but we could have made it more specific and with more datas. However, growth of the business is unparalysed in the company's history.'

The vice-chairman smiled at his use of the word 'unparalysed'. Raj's murder of the English language was the butt of jokes in the boardroom and the vice-chairman filed away this word in his memory, to be repeated at the next board meeting.

Iqbal kept hovering around the vice-chairman's circle of

friends. When the vice-chairman noticed him, he put his hand on Iqbal's shoulder and said, 'So, young man, I hope you are protecting the financial assets of our company.'

Iqbal's chest swelled and he stammered, 'Sir, I assure you that I will do my best.'

'Good,' said the vice-chairman. 'That is what I would have expected of you.' He walked away.

Sangeeta was looking stunning. She had taken particular care with her make-up and hair and had worn a mildly seductive long dress, which was unusual in a room full of ladies wearing sarees.

She was surrounded by a number of male managers in their mid-thirties and early forties. She loved all the attention she was getting, though her eyes kept darting from the chairman to the vice-chairman, hoping one of them would call her. She had been given an opportunity to work very closely with the new chairman while he was the vice-chairman because of his interest in the software business and her body language seemed to suggest that she had a proprietary interest in him.

She had noticed the chairman call Rahul. She had seen the vice-chairman put his arm around Iqbal's shoulder while talking to him, and felt a tinge of jealousy. However, she quickly looked away and went back to the attention she was getting from all the other managers.

Rahul, after his brief interaction with the chairman, was happy chatting with colleagues from his own division. He was a secure individual and though he would also have loved to shake hands with all the top leadership, he chose to stay with his own colleagues and his director. He was comfortable in the fact that he had made an excellent presentation at the critical 'passing the baton' conference.

Anita spent the entire evening sitting on the sidelines with some of the women managers of the company. She was still not confident enough to walk up to the senior managers and chat with them.

Raj had always enjoyed his drink, and his colleagues could see he was not being able to hold himself after three large whiskies. He had started to slur a bit and was a little unsteady on his feet. As Rahul and Sangeeta saw him walk a little shakily towards the chairman again, they walked up to him and casually guided him away to another group of managers from the power division. Rahul stopped the waiter from bringing any more drinks to him.

One of Raj's colleagues put a firm hand on his shoulder and, without giving him an opportunity to make a scene, took him back to his hotel room and tucked him into bed.

The party ended around midnight and everyone made their way back to their rooms, secure in the fact that the new leadership of the company was in place and their future was in the hands of strong leaders, who would guide them well in the new decade and into the new millennium.

~

Rahul

Rahul and Lata were both in their thirties as they started the new decade.

They had started to settle down together and accept each other's idiosyncrasies. Their children now demanded a lot of time, and their parents were also getting older. They were happy together and though they fought like any married couple, they believed that they were fortunate in being able to understand each other, unlike a lot of their friends.

Life seemed good. Rahul's career was going as planned. Their children were doing well. They were taking holidays regularly. Both of them were in good health. Yet, at the back of their minds, they wondered how long this could last. Everything could not stay perfect forever. The bubble had to burst sometime.

As they entered their thirties, they found that it was getting more difficult to lose that extra kilo. Lata exercised regularly in the club gym and Rahul went for a morning walk whenever possible.

Their children had started school and while Rahul missed most of their school events and parent-teacher meetings, he did his best to keep himself updated with their progress by spending time with them over the weekends. He would try and help them with their homework. He would invest as much time as he could with his family, taking them out for regular holidays.

Both the children were good students and always did well in class. While Lata took the major decisions when it came to their education, Rahul was consulted sometimes when he was at home and had the time to listen to such matters. Yet, he always felt guilty about not being present for his family all the time. He always remembered what Lata had told him about his work and he never repeated the statement that he was working for his family.

Why do other couples waltz through life while we face so many problems? both of them would think quite often. Whenever such a thought came, they would both try a little harder to make their marriage work.

They took annual holidays with their children to Disneyland in California and Walt Disney World, Florida. They spent time together in Europe and visited theme parks in Malaysia and Hong Kong. They travelled to Australia and New Zealand. In every country they visited, they would hire a car at the airport and while Rahul would drive, Lata would navigate. Her map-reading skills were excellent and at times like these, they made a great team.

It was during one such holiday to Singapore that Rahul complained to Lata of a mild pain in his jaw and his left shoulder when they returned after a long day of sightseeing. He had started to feel a little heaviness in his arm when he worked out in the hotel gym in the mornings, but had not bothered to heed these warning signals.

Lata had seen her father suffer similar symptoms several years back when he had had a heart attack.

'I am taking you to the hospital right away,' she told Rahul.

'Why don't we wait? We have so many things planned with

the children. Let us not spoil our vacation. Maybe this is a false alarm,' he protested.

Lata refused to listen. She rushed Rahul to a local super specialty hospital. The doctors at the hospital put him through various tests and did an angiogram on him.

'We have found a blockage of over 96 per cent in one of your main arteries,' they told him. 'You need to have a stent put into the blocked artery as quickly as possible to avoid further damage.'

The doctors assured him that this was a simple standard procedure and that he would be fit and ready within a week. They further advised him that it would not be wise to wait until they returned to India, since the blockage was significant and Rahul ran the risk of recurrence, which could cause greater collateral damage.

Lata and Rahul discussed the advice given by the doctors.

'I think you should undergo surgery,' she said. She was always the stronger of the two when it came to decisions related to the health of their family.

He agreed with her.

Jai Hanuman Gyan Gun Sagar
Jai Kapis Tihu Lok Ujagar
Ram Doot Atulit Bal Dhama
Anjani Putra Pavan Sut Nama

The procedure was completed within a couple of hours and Rahul was back in his hotel two days later. The doctors had also told Rahul that he needed to get into a regular exercise regimen and reduce weight. He would need regular annual check-ups to ensure that there would be no recurrence of the complication as well.

'Let us keep this surgery to ourselves and our immediate families,' Lata suggested once he had recovered. 'We don't want anyone in the company to see this as a sign of weakness, lest it hurt your career.'

Lata and Rahul further decided to pay the entire costs of the procedure out of their own pocket, and not claim it either from the insurance company or from Trust Corporation. Neither of them wanted anyone to know about it, just in case senior management felt Rahul would not be fit for higher responsibilities.

'As you become more senior, people will look for excuses to drop you from the race. We have to make sure they do not,' Lata remarked, quoting her father.

~

Lata decided to host a large party for Rahul's fortieth birthday.

She knew that Trust Corporation always supported any activity that would be seen as building stronger bonds within the company. She had special cards printed for the occasion, carefully selected the menu and supervised the decor and arrangements.

She agonized about the colour of the linen on the tables and inspected the uniforms of all the serving staff. The desserts were carefully worked out. She left the arrangements for the bar to Rahul, who asked the local company bootlegger to arrange for 'genuine' Scotch whisky. The rest of the alcohol was obtained through his father's contact from the army canteen supplies depot at significantly lower prices. The background music was selected based on Lata's knowledge of the musical preferences of the chairman's wife.

The party was a resounding success. Most people came early and stayed late into the night.

The chairman and his wife, as well as all the other board members and their spouses, were in attendance. The chairman, who was known to avoid parties usually, stayed almost till the very end. He and his wife were fond of Rahul and Lata.

Raj, Sangeeta, Iqbal and Anita were also invited. All of them came alone.

All their peers as well as some seniors could see that Rahul and Lata had pulled off a minor coup and that Lata had started positioning her husband for the next round of promotions to the board of directors.

~

At the same time, work pressure for Rahul was increasing exponentially.

He had been promoted to deputy general manager as he turned thirty. He was now responsible for meeting the revenue and profit targets of east and northeast India. The market was large. Between 15 to 20 per cent of Indians consumed alcohol and, over the past twenty years, the numbers had increased from one in three hundred to one in twenty. It was estimated that of these, 5 per cent could be classed as alcoholics or alcohol dependent. That translated into approximately five million people addicted to drinking.

Rahul was on the road for at least four days every week, which meant that he would leave home on a Monday morning and return by Friday evening. He knew every distributor of Trust Corporation in his region by name. In several cases, he knew their family members as well. He was as comfortable talking to a salesman as he was while talking to a director.

He performed well and delivered record sales and profits. After two years he was moved to handle the northern region, which was the largest and most profitable for the company. Once again, given his commitment to work and his interpersonal skills, he delivered more than what was expected from him.

There were days when he wondered if he would ever be able to stop running this mad race. He wanted to slow down because his body was giving him signals, but his mind and his heart kept pushing him. He had started running on a treadmill when he had joined the company and now, if he stopped suddenly, he would fall down and get hurt.

After his heart surgery, he knew that he was fit and therefore did not hesitate to push himself. He had to achieve an entry into the corner office. This was a promise he had made to himself.

~

Rahul was very well networked in the parent company in USA. He was always called for a drink whenever the American managers visited India. Lata and Rahul made it a point to go the extra mile to spend time and entertain all overseas visitors.

In order to give him an insight into the international alcohol markets, Rahul was given an opportunity to work on Long Island, New York, for a period of two years. Lata and Rahul, along with their children, moved to Long Island and lived there for that duration. Rahul was very excited to have been given such exposure at an international level.

Once again, Lata was a source of great strength and support. As Rahul travelled all over USA and Europe to get an understanding of the international businesses of the corporation, she took charge of the children and their home as she had done so admirably in New Delhi. After the end of his term, they moved back to New Delhi. Rahul was ready for larger responsibilities in his company's India division and he was happy to be back. Not only had he visited alcohol-manufacturing facilities all over the world but he now knew far more people in the parent company and in their international subsidiaries than any other manager in India.

He recognized how well he was placed to make a pitch for the top job in India.

~

A couple of years before the end of the decade, Rahul was invited to join the board of directors of Trust Corporation, responsible for the alcohol division. His first dream of joining the board of directors had come true.

He had been elevated to this level before his other four batchmates.

He was forty-three years old.

~

Raj

Raj and Lovely had been married for ten years by 1990.

They continued to live apart because Raj did not want anyone to interfere with his lifestyle. Lovely had grown used to being without Raj and staying with his parents in Chandigarh. Her children were her only source of joy. She had built a small 'kitty' group in the city with women of her age. They would meet regularly in different restaurants every week and discuss husbands, in-laws and children.

With all the heavy food at every meal and no exercise, Lovely had put on over thirty kilos since her marriage. She now weighed an obese eighty-six kilos and was comfortable with it, thinking she had no reason to lose weight.

'I don't believe in dieting. Who should I lose weight for? In any case, no one will look at me,' was her standard line to her kitty group friends.

Raj was a good provider to his family and would regularly send money every month. Money was the main link between him and his family. He would call his children and his parents every week. However, he would discuss his children's school reports with his father, not with his wife. Though he did speak to Lovely during his weekly calls, their conversation was very basic.

'How are you?' Raj would ask.

'I am well. I hope you are eating properly?' Lovely would respond.

'Yes, I am eating well. How is your health?' he would enquire to which she would reply, 'Fine, talk to the children,' and hand over the phone.

Both knew that they would repeat the same words the next week and the following. They had never been close but as the years passed, they became virtual strangers. What held them together in their marriage were their children and Raj's parents.

On one of Raj's trips to Mumbai, he bumped into his old secretary and flame Barbara in the lobby of the hotel he was staying at. She had been his first indiscretion after marriage and he had always missed her, though he had never stopped his philandering.

'How nice to meet you, Barbara, where have you been all these days?' he said warmly, forgetting how he had treated her and how he had been instrumental in getting her fired.

'I now live in Mumbai. I have a son who is eight years old and I have just separated from my husband,' she replied.

Barbara did not tell him that her child was a result of her affair with Raj. He'd had her fired before she could tell him anything and she had never forgotten this embarrassment. She had had to leave the city because of the false charges made against her. Though she was aware of his faults and knew that he had wronged her, there was a powerful attraction that she still felt for him.

However, this time she was determined to be more cautious. So she decided to record all their conversations on her mobile phone. She had followed his career closely and was aware that he was a senior manager in Trust Corporation and rising very quickly. She also knew that he was earning well and the rumour mill was active about the extra money he was making from suppliers.

Raj, too, recognized the attraction between them and asked her out for dinner that evening. She accepted immediately. After dinner, when he proposed that she come to his room for a nightcap, she took his hand and agreed. They fell into each other's arms and hungrily devoured one another.

'Oh Raj! How much I have thought of you, and how much I have missed you,' she whispered into his ear as they lay together on his bed.

'Never leave me again. You are too precious for me,' he replied, holding her close.

Raj thought he had found a diversion for himself in Mumbai. Barbara believed she had found her life insurance. Both of them promised to meet in his hotel every time he was in the city.

Till I get tired of you again, he thought.

Till I fix you and extract enough out of you to look after myself and your child for the rest of my life, she thought.

Raj had continued his heavy smoking and drinking and was quite unfit, with an emerging potbelly. He used to experience aches and pains in his legs and back, but he had always chosen to ignore his body. He loved to quote Mark Twain when he was asked about how much he exercised.

'Every time I feel like exercising, I lie down till the feeling passes,' he would smirk.

During one of his sojourns with Barbara in Mumbai, after some intense and very satisfying sex, Raj felt some discomfort in his chest and broke out in a cold sweat. There was a dull pain in his jaw too. His eyes rolled back in their sockets and his breathing became laboured. Barbara knew immediately that there was something wrong with him.

'Call the doctor, Barbara,' he whispered in a voice that sent a shiver down her spine. She was not ready to lose him so soon.

She called the reception and asked for the hotel doctor to rush to his room.

The doctor saw him a few minutes later and told him, 'You need to be moved to a hospital immediately. You have just had a mild heart attack. I am going to give you a sedative till you reach the hospital.'

Raj could not believe that this was happening to him.

The first thought that crossed his mind was what Lovely would say when she found out that he was with a woman in a hotel room when he had a heart attack. His second thought was that his company would see him as a weak person after his illness. He was not able to think any further, since the sedative he had been given put him to sleep.

In the hospital his condition was stabilized, and after all the tests were completed, the doctors decided that he needed multiple coronary bypasses, since three of his arteries were severely blocked.

Raj's parents had passed away a few years back and had left their entire wealth and property to Lovely. They had realized that their son had been unfair to his wife and children. Lovely, for the first time, started to feel secure now that she owned some assets.

Lovely and the children joined Raj in Mumbai when he had his surgery. He asked Barbara to stay away from the hospital while his family was with him.

He was advised by his cardiologist to change his lifestyle completely. He would need to change his food habits, lose some weight, stop smoking, reduce his alcohol consumption and get into a regular exercise routine.

Lovely took him back to Chandigarh and nursed him back to health. She managed his food carefully and made him go for regular walks. Raj enjoyed spending time with his children but he was essentially a loner and soon started to feel that his life was being intruded into, even by his immediate family.

Lovely knew that he would never come back completely into her life, but she valued the time she was able to spend with him in the few weeks that he was convalescing. She was also aware of his affair with Barbara. She had been told by the hotel doctor about the lady who had been with Raj in his room when the doctor had visited him. However, in order to avoid a scene with her husband, Lovely chose to keep quiet.

She was completely unaware of Barbara's son, though.

While Raj did pledge to Lovely that he would change his lifestyle after his surgery, he followed his new routine only for a few months. Once he started work and had to travel again, he was back to his drinking. He did give up smoking though, because he was convinced that had been the primary cause of his heart attack.

It took him only a short while to go back to Barbara.

Barbara encouraged him to drink with her because she felt that this was one way to hold on to him. She also started spending more time with him in his hotel room each time he was in Mumbai.

Raj had now started drinking even more heavily. Every evening he would stare at his watch till it was 7.30 p.m. and then pour himself a stiff whisky. From consuming two drinks every night when he was in his thirties, he was drinking over six large pegs every evening by the time he was in his early forties. After this, he would fall asleep on the chair in a drunken stupor and be put into his bed by Barbara or by an attentive housekeeping staff member.

Raj also had to travel extensively all over Southeast Asia looking at power plants. He would spend a lot of time in every hotel bar and soon made friends with several barmen. He was a generous tipper, so they would sometimes slip him an extra drink free of cost. As he drank more and more, he would talk to them about various subjects. They were trained to listen to their customers and not offer any comment in return.

'I have had a lousy marriage,' he would tell some people.

'I must make it as the chairman of the company, but I am nervous of Sangeeta and Rahul,' he would tell others.

'I have so much money that I can buy anything I want,' he would boast at some places.

'I am so unhappy. Nothing in my life has turned out the way I wanted,' he would mourn.

His barmen friends also became his steady source for women.

His need for sex almost every night started to get more pronounced after his heart surgery. As soon as he had checked into a hotel in a new city, he would first reach out for the local yellow pages directory and flip to the 'Escorts and Massage' section. Raj indulged in most of his sexual activities without any protection and it was not long before he contracted syphilis.

He also infected Barbara.

'You bastard!' she shouted, when she found out. 'Why can't you stop sleeping with whores everywhere? Why have you infected me with this horrible disease?'

'I don't sleep with anyone other than you,' Raj shouted back. 'You must have contracted this from one of your many lovers and given it to me, and now you are blaming me.'

He refused to get himself tested. Barbara, too, had a bigger plan to extract money from him, so she went back to sleeping with him once both of them had been cured.

He would tell his friends at the bar after drinking, 'I am not sure how long my runway is now. I must make best of my remaining active life.'

He would randomly call an escort and ask her to leave immediately after his needs had been satiated. He did not think about the girl after she had left his room and he never called the same person a second time. His appetite for women was insatiable and his phonebook had numbers of pimps in all the major cities of India and Southeast Asia.

He would often tell the girls who visited him, 'I never pay to have sex. I pay you to leave my room afterwards.'

The girls just wanted his money. They did not really care about the raving and ranting of a drunken man.

~

India was perpetually short of power to meet its agricultural, industrial, commercial and residential needs. State-owned and privately-owned companies were significant players in the country's electricity sector, with the private sector growing at a faster rate.

India's central government and state governments jointly regulated the electricity sector. The new government formed in 1991, with Prime Minister Narasimha Rao, had promised liberalization of the power sector. Within the first five years of the new decade, Indian businesses committed to invest over ₹2,75,000 crore and generate over 75,000 crore MW. The Government of India had always used power as a political tool by providing free power for agriculture. In addition, more than one-third of the power generated in India was lost or stolen.

The transmission network was not the only vulnerable part of the power supply chain, which was one giant bottleneck. Frequent blackouts were common. As a result most large companies, residential complexes, shopping complexes and even India's airports had backup generators or their own mini-power stations. Most local distribution firms were state-owned and all but bankrupt, as politicians insisted that tariffs stay low and big swathes of the population, including farmers, get free power.

Many Indians got away by simply stealing power to light up their fancy farmhouses or homes. The main thefts were generally ascribed to the rich and famous, and they did so brazenly. No one had the courage to unhook the illegal wiretap on the main power cable outside the rows of huge farmhouses in various cities.

Trust Corporation had announced plans to double its power capacity. The company had primarily concentrated on hydel power for the last ten years but now it started looking at thermal, solar and wind generating options. It was a large player in nuclear power in its international plants, but this option was not open to the private sector in India.

Liberalization of power brought a lot of bureaucratic and political controls, and interference in the garb of opening up of the economy. As a major investor in this sector, Trust Corporation was the first choice for the government. Raj, on behalf of his company, was in the lead for all discussions.

In order to get the company's proposals cleared by the government, Raj would spend a lot of time and money on bureaucrats and politicians. He negotiated all deals with politicians directly and had worked out a simple system of keeping 10 per cent of all the money he had to pay. He justified this to himself, saying that he was negotiating much better directly rather than through a middleman.

In addition to setting up new plants and negotiating with the central and state governments, Raj was also required to source coal for the company's ever-hungry thermal power plant. Coal was completely controlled by the mafia and the politicians. Getting access to good quality coal to ensure that their plants ran without trouble and at the highest efficiency levels needed political sanction, for which large payoffs had to be made to political parties. Trust Corporation empowered Raj to handle this, and unknowingly gave Raj an opportunity to make even more money than earlier. Procurement of coal gave him a lucrative chance to collect a further 10 per cent for his personal use with no one the wiser, since all that he was required to do was to approve substandard coal from the suppliers.

True to its name, Trust Corporation trusted its senior managers, and no one ever thought that they had a manager in their midst who could be stealing from the company. Given his direct and intimate contacts with bureaucrats and politicians, Raj was able to get approvals very quickly, and his company acknowledged and rewarded his performance.

Raj was generating so much cash through his 10 per cent route that he struggled to manage it. After literally throwing away money in what could be called conspicuous consumption at its extreme, he still had huge cash surpluses. Leaving so much money at home was dangerous. He decided to take Lovely into confidence about all the surplus cash he was generating, without telling her the source.

'Lovely, I am making a lot of money now and I want you to handle all this cash for our family,' he told her on one of his visits.

'If it is all cash, how will I keep it at home?' she asked. After giving it some thought she suggested, 'I will invest all the cash you give me into land.'

Lovely was delighted to play a small part in her husband's life. Raj agreed to her suggestion and started to accumulate land and other fixed assets in third-party names. Lovely started managing this property portfolio for him.

Raj knew that this was a risky transaction; if the benami holder of the land went against him, the land would be lost. However, since he had no other options, he had to go along with his wife and make these investments. He had always assumed that she was a simple middle-class woman who would do everything that he would ask her to.

But Lovely saw an opportunity in this to gain financial security for herself. Given the philandering ways of her husband, she was always unsure of when her monthly cheque would be stopped. So she purchased the land in a series of names unknown to Raj but under her direct control.

Lovely's life now changed as well. From a situation where she would wait for the monthly remittance from Raj, which would arrive by the twentieth of each month, she now had more cash in her purse than she had ever had before. Raj's allowance had lost its relevance, except when she had to pay off some expenses by cheque.

She started increasing the contribution to her kitty parties. Then she began playing cards with her friends and her stake started to increase exponentially. When her friends found it difficult to cope with her stakes, she abandoned the group and looked for richer friends. She would lose ₹20,000 in one day and pay the money with a flourish. She would always say, 'My day to win will come' and to be fair to her, she did win quite often. She also started to entertain more and more at home and made new friends.

All her repressed feelings were now surfacing as she gained acceptance into the most elite society parties of the city. Her newfound wealth surprised the conservative social circles in Chandigarh, but as always happens in India, no one ever questioned it. Everyone was in for the ride.

'Who are we to stop a middle-aged wealthy woman from throwing her money around?' was the common statement made by everyone invited to her parties.

~

Rumours had started floating around in the hallowed corridors of Trust Corporation that Raj had wealth beyond his means. There were hushed conversations about how he was making so much money. However, no one had any evidence and as long as he was getting the work done, it was not thought necessary to question him. Besides, Raj was very well connected politically and no one wanted to jeopardize the political relationships he had built for the company.

Raj was promoted to executive vice-president in charge of the power division by the end of the decade, reporting directly to the vice-chairman. He had hoped that he would also be appointed a director like Rahul and Iqbal, and was disappointed that while he had been given independent charge of the power division, he had not been elevated to the main board. However, he decided to make the most of his position as the head of the power division.

'At least I now have a clear and unquestioned opportunity to make money,' he thought to himself.

He was forty-four years old.

~

Sangeeta

For Sangeeta, her thirties were a time for rejuvenation and excitement. She was single, carefree and independent. She had no strings attached, so she could choose what to do and who to spend time with.

She had read of a study that concluded that it took years of experimenting before women found a look they were happy and confident with. Most felt they were in their prime as they entered their thirties. One in three grew more comfortable with their appearance as they got older, while three out of four thought that their style had improved over the years.

Sangeeta was in the right zone.

She was comfortable being single. Her worry about being a social outcast in her twenties, which was what had encouraged her to marry Ajay Sharma in the first place, was now over.

Her body had filled out and through a regular regimen of exercise and careful eating, her weight was under control. Her improved sense of dressing through extensive overseas travel had accentuated her hourglass figure. Wherever she went, she knew that heads would turn with the words 'Wow, look at her' on the lips of most men. She loved all the attention she was getting.

Her parents had tried their best to dissuade her from getting a divorce. But she had been adamant, citing reasons like incompatibility and lack of attention, and though they did not understand her reasons, they supported her nonetheless. They found reasons to explain the divorce to their friends and extended family, who blamed Sangeeta's 'foreign education' for her 'Western outlook'.

'What else could we have expected from a girl who has studied in America?' her older relatives would comment. 'This is all because her father did not listen to us and sent her alone to study abroad.'

'What is the use of being so broad-minded if it destroys your daughter's home?' other relatives would say, blaming her parents.

'She is an American citizen, so obviously she will do what she has learned there,' remarked an old aunt.

When her mother suggested that Sangeeta consider getting married again and start a family, she replied, 'Ma, you know that I will never be able to marry again. You should also understand that I will not have any time to bring up children. I am happy as I am.'

She had been through one failed marriage and was not willing to invest her time and energy into another one, or accept the moods and requirements of a permanent man in her life. Her goal was no longer a lifetime of love, companionship and shared experiences. She wanted an occasional meeting with a young man, with perhaps a short-term commitment for a few weeks or months, to keep things interesting in her life.

Besides, she had no time from her work.

~

Sangeeta was regular with her medical check-ups. She was generally very fit, regular with her morning walks and used the treadmill in the club gym or the hotel where she was staying at least thrice a week.

As she turned thirty-seven, during her annual tests, the doctors did a mammogram. They found a large lump inside her left breast.

'It could be breast cancer,' her doctor told her, sending a chill down her spine.

They asked her to go through a series of scans and diagnosed the lump as a tumour. They took a sample of the tumour for further testing. As she waited a couple of days for her results, her mind was numbed into thinking why God was being so unkind to her.

The biopsy results came back and the doctor told her, 'I am sorry to inform you that the test is positive and the tumour is malignant. We should schedule a surgery very quickly to avoid further growth, as well as to prevent it from metastasizing into other parts of the body.'

Sangeeta was shaken by this information.

Since she had never trusted anyone and did not have any friends, she had no one to speak to except her parents. She wished she had the strong assured voice of Ajay, her ex-husband, for support but quickly shut this thought from her mind.

'That is a closed chapter and I must never become weak about him again,' she told herself.

She called her parents and told them about her condition. After the initial shock, they came to live with her in New Delhi. She had always been very conscious of her looks and her body, so it was natural for her to ask the doctor if her breast would have a scar after the surgery.

'I don't want an ugly scar and I do not want anyone to know that I have had surgery,' she said.

The doctor assured her that the scar from the surgery would be hidden in the fold of the breast. She underwent the operation and the doctors removed a three-centimetre lump from her breast. They also removed some of the breast tissue and some lymph nodes. The test results came back, and fortunately for her, the cancer had not spread into the tissue surrounding the tumour and her lymph nodes were clear. There was no sign of the cancer having spread anywhere else in her body.

The doctor told her that she was fine after her surgery and recommended an annual mammogram.

'You are very fortunate that we caught this early,' he said.

Sangeeta was a healthy young woman and she recovered her strength very quickly. Within a couple of weeks she was back at work. However, sleep started to elude her. She travelled extensively and sleep became a precious commodity. Her body always craved more sleep and the more she thought about it, the longer she would lie awake at night. The doctor advised her to start taking a mild sedative. Before she realized it, she had increased her dosage substantially without the doctor's advice and very soon she was dependent on the sleeping tablets.

After her surgery, Sangeeta went from one relationship to another. She had beaten cancer and her desire to lead a full life returned with zest and vigour. She would attract men towards her like bees to honey and she would use them and discard them when she was satiated. Her conscience never bothered her when she agreed to sleep with a man. For her, this was a simple contract for a short period of time to satisfy physical needs. She was absolutely clear that there would never be any emotional involvement with anyone.

On one of her travels, she had been introduced to an airline pilot, Arun, who was in his early forties. He was also a divorcee and they started meeting whenever possible.

Both enjoyed the time they spent together and both did not expect any commitment. If they happened to be in the same city, she would make sure she booked herself in the same hotel as him and they would spend the night together. The next day, he would take his aircraft wherever it was scheduled to go and she would carry on with her work.

Arun provided the anchor in her life that had been missing since her separation from Ajay. She slowed down seeing other men and would wait to meet him whenever feasible.

Sangeeta's life was often discussed by the leadership of the company and though it was her personal life, a conservative top management steeped in old American culture was sometimes paranoid about what the rest of the world would think. However, since Sangeeta was performing well, these 'transgressions', as the company saw them, were ignored. Anita, though, was aware of these discussions and she tried to warn Sangeeta.

'Sangeeta, I think you need to do some introspection about your personal life. This is now becoming a matter of discussion in the boardroom,' she told her friend.

'Anita, I think you should mind your own business. Look at your life with your husband. People who live in glass houses should not throw stones,' Sangeeta responded sharply.

Anita spoke no further.

However, the management, in one of their internal assessments of future leaders, made a note that further leadership roles for Sangeeta would be discussed very seriously, keeping in mind her personal life.

Sangeeta is not setting the right example for the younger managers, was recorded in her personal file.

Anita chose to say nothing to Sangeeta about this. Serves her right, she thought.

~

The software division of the company had grown by leaps and bounds in the 1980s.

It had been an anticipatory move by the top management and this division would continue to bear a lot of fruit in the decades to come. The 1990s brought its own set of challenges, as several Indian companies started offering the same set of services, which were highly qualified young engineers at significantly lower salaries as compared to those of Trust Corporation.

Indeed, the 1990s was a decade of virtual revolution, with commercial web browsers taking over. Communication saw a new dawn and collaboration increased exponentially. With more bandwidth available and the cost of hardware steadily coming down, the globe became better represented on the World Wide Web, providing a level playing field for everyone.

15 August 1995 was a milestone in the life of the young software business in India. The Internet was initially introduced in New Delhi, Mumbai, Chennai and Pune. The success of this sector was largely attributed to the lack of government interference.

Sangeeta had to travel to various parts of Europe and USA virtually fifteen days every month to drum up more and more business for the company. Her international travel was a source of a lot of jealousy amongst her peers, since they knew that she was able to save foreign exchange from her allowance, which, when converted into rupees was a tidy sum every month.

However, not many people could say anything to her, partly because she was delivering excellent results, and partly because this business had the blessings of the chairman and the vice-chairman.

Sangeeta had her own ways of getting business contracts. She believed in getting her work done, no matter what the cost.

She had been chasing one client in USA for several months. It had become imperative for her to get this contract, not because of its value but because she would acquire this client from another major Indian company. Once she got her appointment and made her presentation to the company vice-president, she invited him out for a drink. She saw the wedding band on his finger but was determined to do whatever it took to get the contract.

After a couple of glasses of wine and an expensive dinner, he offered to drop her back to her hotel.

'Why don't you come up to my suite for a drink?' she said when they reached the hotel.

Intrigued by this beautiful woman, who promised much more than she was communicating to him, he went up with her to her room. Sangeeta had planned the evening carefully. She had pre-ordered a bottle of champagne.

The two of them wound up in her bed.

By the time she woke up with a heavy head, he had gone but left his phone number on a paper napkin on her bedside table. When she met him again the following day at work he did not make any eye contact with her.

Sangeeta got the software contract and was applauded by the chairman when she returned to India.

She continued meeting the vice-president as long as he had the ability to give her new contracts or renew existing ones. She had no compunction in calling him over to her room after work and spending the night with him. However, the day he was sidelined in his company and had to resign from his job, she dropped him and never took any calls from him again.

Her big learning after this relationship was that she could use her charms quite easily for her company and for her own growth. She never hesitated in doing so thereafter.

By 1999, she was heading all the markets of the software division and had been promoted to the rank of executive vice-president, software, reporting directly to the vice-chairman in charge of the division.

Like Raj, she too had hoped that she would be appointed to the board of directors but it was felt by the management that she was not ready. She had not learned to lose and had always managed to get whatever she wanted, personally or professionally. This setback in her career, as she saw it, was difficult for her to accept. However, she swallowed her anger and frustration and vowed to work even harder than before.

She also found it hard to accept that two of her batchmates, Rahul and Iqbal, had been elevated to the board of directors before her. She agonized over what had gone wrong and why she had not been found ready. However, she took comfort in the fact that Raj and Anita had not yet been elevated to the board.

She was one of only two women at her level in the history of Trust Corporation. The other was Anita Fernandes.

She was forty-one years old.

~

Iqbal

Samina and Iqbal had an uncomfortable relationship of mutual acceptance.

He never commented on how she was looking, nor did he ever notice what clothes or jewellery she wore. They had nothing to talk about except their children and food. He did not like her wearing any make-up and she killed her desire to look good within a couple of years of marriage. Though she was a beautiful woman, she made herself look ordinary and slunk into a corner of the room whenever she met any friends.

Iqbal, like Raj and Rahul, loved food and had never believed in exercising. As he approached his thirties, he started to put on weight.

'What's for dinner?' was the first question he asked Samina every evening as he came home from work.

By the time he reached his mid-thirties, his weight was over 90 kilos and by the time he was forty, he had reached an uncomfortable 105 kilos. He had to sleep on his back all the time since he was not able to sleep on his side. His asthma had started acting up again because of his excessive weight. He felt out of breath while walking up the one flight of steps to his office. He was not able to run up the steps for an urgent meeting and had to wait for the elevator.

Soon his knees started to give trouble. He walked with a slight slouch since most of his weight was centred on his shoulders and his waist. His head reached out in front of his body like a duck because he was subconsciously trying to balance the excessive weight around his waist. He also walked like a duck, waddling his way through. His hands and fingers too had gained in size and he was not able to close his hands into a fist. He could no longer wear his wedding ring.

Samina was also not careful in what she ate. She had let her own body and weight slide after Iqbal lost interest in her. She had put on twenty-five kilos after the delivery of her three sons.

She would make heavy fried food for lunch and dinner, and always ensure a tasty dessert after every meal. The two of them had never had much in common and food became a passion for both. 'The best way to a man's heart is through his stomach' was what she had been taught by her mother before she had been married. Samina had done everything within her power to adhere to this.

When Iqbal turned forty-two, he went for his first medical check-up, after being given an ultimatum by Anita. Iqbal had always believed that it was better not to go for a check-up since it was more convenient to not know what was going on inside him than to worry.

'I am okay, Anita. Don't bother about my health,' he said.

'Iqbal, you are required to go for an annual medical check-up and if you don't have it done immediately, I will have no option but to put a note in your personal file,' Anita replied.

The doctor was shocked to see this rotund man, looking much older than his years, struggling to walk inside his clinic.

It took a while for the lab technician to find his vein to draw the blood for his blood tests. At the treadmill test, the technician had to stop the machine after four minutes since Iqbal had reached his maximum heartbeat. Normally the test should have continued for fifteen minutes. His liver test showed a fatty liver. His cholesterol levels were high and his triglycerides had touched record levels. What surprised the doctor most were his HbA1c levels, at 15.2. He was clearly a diabetic.

'Diabetes, coupled with high blood pressure and excessive obesity, is a killer, Mr Mohammad,' the doctor said. 'You have to lose 20 kilos immediately, otherwise I cannot promise that you will be able to stay in good health for a long period of time. You are a walking time bomb and you have to take charge of your health right now.'

When Iqbal returned home, Samina asked him about his test results. He took the easy way out and blamed her for all his faults, as he had done throughout his married life.

'You have made me diabetic,' he accused. 'You have given me high blood pressure. My cholesterol is out of control. What else will you do to me? If you had been careful about the food you had given me, I would not have been in the situation I am in now!'

Once again, Samina accepted the blame for his illness and told him that she would change the food she gave him. She knew deep inside that he would never change his food habits and she would have to keep bearing his tantrums.

~

Iqbal turned to God after his illness.

He had led a simple, straight life and had always been God-fearing. He knew that he had been unkind to his family but he did not think he had done anything wrong to them. He saw himself as a good husband and a good father. He had provided for all their needs.

He also started to spend a lot of time with preachers in the local mosque. He had been brought up in a conservative Muslim household and it was natural for him to turn to religion as he grew older. He would say his prayers five times a week and had managed to get the HR department to create a separate room in the head office, where Muslim staff members could go for their daily prayers.

Though women are allowed to pray in a mosque, Iqbal preferred that Samina pray at home. He also insisted that his sons learn all the prayers and participate in the religious functions.

On 6 December 1992, when the sixteenth-century Babri Masjid in Ayodhya was torn down by workers of the Vishwa Hindu Parishad, Iqbal felt for the first time in his life that this was an attack on him and his religion. The realization also dawned on him that he belonged to a minority community. He had never ever felt alienated in his own country and this was surprising for him. Some of his closest colleagues were Hindus, Sikhs and Christians, yet he agonized over why he felt so much anger against Hindus.

Iqbal recognized that as an employee of a major multinational company, he could not do much for his religion without jeopardizing his career. He suppressed his anger, though his colleagues sensed a change in him.

He would express his frustration to Samina but since they had never had a discussion on any matter other than food, she was not able to have an intelligent conversation with him on this subject.

His next best solution to support the cause of the community was to provide funds. He started giving large donations to the mosque from his salary without telling anyone. He also chose not to ask anyone in the mosque what his money would be used for.

~

Iqbal had assumed that since his mentor, the former finance director, had now become the vice-chairman of the company, Iqbal would get additional favours from him.

However this was not to be. While the vice-chairman had always had a soft spot for Iqbal, he had his own reputation to protect and wanted to be seen as an impartial leader.

'You will have to find your own feet, old chap,' said the vice-chairman once. 'Don't expect any undue favours from me. On the contrary, I will be much tougher with you, given that we have worked together in the past.'

The top managers of the company had been known to stay away from any favouritism. As the finance director, the vice-chairman had enjoyed interacting with Iqbal and hearing rumours and gossip from him. As the vice-chairman, he had a much larger canvas to look at. Besides, Iqbal was now reporting to the new finance director and had to learn to sink or swim on his own.

Iqbal's brilliance with numbers was unparalleled within the company, and the entire board of directors started to rely increasingly on him. He was also considered their resident expert on taxes.

Since alcohol was a very heavily taxed product in the country, Iqbal took this on as his first challenge. Through a complex set of financial structuring deals, he managed to create several pack sizes resulting in lower tax burdens and hence a better price for the consumer. This single move led to a major increase in the company's revenues and profits.

He then addressed the challenge of the huge depreciation that would accrue from the investments made in the power business. Working with leading tax authorities, he was able to capitalize projects in a manner that the depreciation benefit to the company was the maximum possible.

'These structures are very tax-efficient and the government is actually paying for a large part of our projects through tax savings that are accruing to the company,' he would tell the board of directors.

The third business of the company, software, was export-led. Iqbal once again worked with top accountants and lawyers and managed to get export incentives for the company, in addition to tax rebates, by setting off previous year losses of the division against profits from the alcohol division.

The combined result of his financial re-engineering was amazing.

Through sheer brilliance and financial acumen, Iqbal had increased the profits of the company by 2 percentage points. This was a very significant achievement and was acknowledged by the chairman and vice-chairman of the company in an open board meeting, where Iqbal was given a standing ovation.

By the late 1990s, Iqbal had been promoted to chief financial officer and everyone spoke about his becoming the next finance director of Trust Corporation.

When Rahul was appointed to the board, the vice-chairman felt that the finance function should not be weakened and he pushed for the appointment of Iqbal as the next finance director.

The chairman, who was stepping down the following

year, accepted the recommendation of his colleague and communicated this to the shareholders. The shareholders accepted the proposal and by the turn of the century, Iqbal was elevated to the position of finance director.

He was forty-four years old.

~

Anita

Life for Anita and Michael had changed significantly after the arrival of their daughter.

Michael was a completely different man with the baby in the house. While he still did not work and depended on Anita to pay for all his expenses, he took complete charge of their home and their child. He would wake up early and ensure that the maids had packed Anita's lunch by 8 a.m. when she left for work. He would drop their daughter to school and sit with her to complete her homework. Anita wondered whether he was repenting for his earlier wild life, and whether this change was permanent or a passing phase. She had never been able to understand her husband and this new behaviour made her happy, yet wary at the same time.

He was also willingly going to church with her, unlike the early days when he would sleep late on Sundays and she would go to church to pray for both of them.

'I think we should admit our daughter into Sunday school,' suggested Michael one day.

Anita agreed immediately, grateful to her husband for making the suggestion. She had gone to Sunday school as a child and knew that the teachers would inculcate good Christian values in their daughter.

Michael was also drinking lesser than he used to, though he had not given up this vice completely. If Anita ever asked him to stop drinking, he would simply state, 'I enjoy my drink every evening. I don't have much else to look forward to.'

Michael was ten years older than Anita. While he had been a fitness freak when they got married, he had stopped working out after their daughter was born. Since he had no physical activity other than household work and looking after their daughter, he was quite unfit. His medical check-ups normally showed elevated cholesterol and sugar levels, but he refused to change his lifestyle.

One evening when Anita returned from office, she was surprised to find him sitting in the rocking chair, his head slumped to one side. Initially she thought he was sleeping, but when he did not respond to her, she walked up to him and touched his shoulder. He looked up slowly, then down again.

Her first reaction was, 'Have you been drinking again, Michael?'

He did not respond and Anita realized that something was wrong with him. She stared at him closely and saw that he was trying to say something to her. His speech was incoherent. She could see that he was trying to lift his arm but was unable to do so. His eyes were looking glassily at her.

She called the company doctor in a state of panic.

'Help me, doctor! Something is seriously wrong with my husband.'

The doctor arrived within an hour and moved Michael to a hospital immediately. As a senior manager in the HR function, Anita had quicker access to medical facilities than other managers, simply because she was responsible for paying all the medical bills for the company managers. She was also in charge of appointing doctors as company retainers.

Michael had suffered a stroke and needed immediate care.

The doctors diagnosed that he'd had several silent strokes in the past few months. As she thought back she remembered him often complaining of numbness in his hands and sometimes a debilitating headache. Each time she had suggested that they go see a doctor, he had always waved his hand and dismissed the headaches as 'nothing serious'.

Life after the stroke changed completely for both of them.

What had been a self-sustaining and enjoyable lifestyle prior to the stroke would no longer be the same. Anita's life altered completely as she found herself in the role of a caregiver. She had been so engrossed in her work after Michael had taken charge of their home and their daughter that she had forgotten what it took to look after a family member.

In addition to the office, where more time was being demanded of her by the company, she now had the added responsibility of looking after her daughter and her husband. In her quiet, self-assured manner she took on all these additional responsibilities without uttering one word of complaint.

She nursed Michael back to health over the next twelve months.

Like most victims of a stroke, Michael stopped whatever little work he was doing at home; nor did he socialize any more. His confidence in himself dropped and so did his self-esteem. He stopped looking after their daughter as he used to and much as Anita would have liked to, she was not able to find the time to look after their child, who was left to be brought up by maidservants.

Though he recovered most of his bodily functions, Michael was a picture of self-pity. Everything was about him and how unkind God had been to him. Anita would read out parts of the Holy Bible to give him comfort, though he never seemed to hear anything. He would tell her, 'I had never believed in retribution. However, now I think that God is punishing me for all the things I should have done in my life, but never did.'

'Hush, my darling. You have been a wonderful husband to me,' she would respond gently. No words could quell his anger against God, though.

Anita went through her annual medical examination without any problem. All her parameters were clear. Her blood pressure was normal, her weight was under control and her blood sugar level was normal.

Her health and fitness irked Michael no end. He blamed himself for not staying in shape and was also angry with his wife for not doing enough to keep him healthy.

That was when he started to take out his anger and frustration on Anita. He shouted at her every time she did not understand what he was trying to say. This traumatized their little daughter, who had never seen her father like that.

~

At work, Anita was extremely busy.

The company had decided to implement a new set of terms and conditions for all its employees. This meant a lot of research on companies of similar size and business.

This was the first major exercise that Anita was spearheading independently with a team of three young managers from her department to support her. She was working directly with the director of human resources for this sensitive and critical exercise. She knew she had to work fast and keep all information confidential. Yet, having spent over two decades in the company, she knew that 'corridor gossip' and lunchtime chats between secretaries would leak some news. This information would seldom be correct but would be enough to keep expectations high and rumours floating all over the company.

The rumour mill was agog with what to expect in the new terms and conditions. Every time a new number was floated, it was debated hotly by the employees and compared with the inflation in the country. Different locations of the company had different views on it.

Employees in Mumbai and Delhi felt that they had to bear a higher burden in terms of cost of living as compared to employees in the power plants in rural Himachal Pradesh. On the other hand, employees in the power plants and alcohol factories felt that they were living in remote locations and should therefore be compensated more as compared to their colleagues, who were based in the larger metro cities.

Everyone had a view when it came to their own performance and compensation. The longer it took for the terms and conditions review committee to arrive at a set of recommendations for the board of directors, the higher the expectations became.

'We can easily expect a 10 per cent hike,' said one employee, based on what he claimed was insider information.

A few weeks later, the number had increased to 12.5 per cent. By now, 10 per cent was the minimum according to the grapevine, with a strong possibility of the number going up.

By the time Anita had completed her recommendations to the board and got them to sign off on the revised terms, six months had elapsed. The rumours were now of increments ranging between 25 and 30 per cent.

When the board approved a hefty 20 per cent increase in

salary levels across the board, there was a general sense of disappointment within the organization.

However, Anita was recognized by the board for all her hard work and for the successful implementation of a major review of terms. Her quiet and efficient manner of working was appreciated by the senior leadership.

She had been slowly moving up the corporate ladder through a series of fortunate developments. Two senior managers had resigned and one fell ill and had to go on long medical leave. Thus, Anita found herself very near the top of her function in the company.

Her journey had been quite uneventful over the past two decades, but no one could take away the fact that she had survived and risen.

By the turn of the decade, she was promoted to the level of executive vice-president, human resources, reporting directly to the chairman. She and Sangeeta were the only two women who had made it to this exalted management level in the history of the company.

She was forty-four years old.

~

The Third Decade

In 1998 India had become a nuclear power and with the onset of the millenium, in 2001, it became the second nation to cross a population of one billion. China had crossed this mark in 1979, one year before the five management trainees started working for Trust Corporation.

There was a newfound confidence after ten years of liberalization. Prime Minister Atal Behari Vajpayee was pushing the agenda of opening up the economy. The country was responding to his positive moves with excitement. Vajpayee conceded that Tibet was an integral part of China; he also entered into a milestone civilian nuclear agreement with George Bush.

Priyanka Chopra became Miss World and Lara Dutta Miss Universe. Abhinav Bindra won India's first individual gold medal in shooting at the Beijing Olympics.

In 2004, the National Democratic Alliance lost the general elections; after Sonia Gandhi did not accept the post, Dr Manmohan Singh was appointed the prime minister of India. Sonia Gandhi was elected as the leader of the United Progressive Alliance. In 2008, a terror attack on a never-seen-before scale was carried out in Mumbai. The political leadership, as it has always done, vowed to do everything in their power to bring the perpetrators to justice. Nothing significant was done of course, after the first comments about the spirit of Mumbai had quelled the anger of the people.

The new millennium started with a lot of positive energy for the country. Investments were flowing in, GDP growth was over 8.5 per cent and the analysts were talking about India averaging a growth of 9.5 per cent for the next decade.

~

Out of the 1980 batch of five management trainees, twenty years later, two had been elevated to the main board of directors and three were heading businesses and functions independently.

This was not a bad track record for HR. They had selected well and justifiably, they had a reason to feel proud of themselves. It was very seldom that the entire batch of selected candidates did so well, proving that the batch of 1980 had been exceptional.

At the turn of the millennium, the vice-chairman of the company was elevated to the position of chairman. The company now had a finance person to lead it into the new millennium.

Once again, as in the previous transitions at the level of chairman, there was churning amongst the board of directors. Every chairman wanted people he could trust around him and his first objective normally was to remove all his peers who might pose a threat at a later date.

Iqbal Mohammad, a financial genius, was appointed the finance director of the company. The director-in-charge of the alcohol division was replaced by Rahul Jain.

Promotions had also been planned in the power division with Raj Dhingra as the head; in the software division, Sangeeta Malhotra and in the human resources function, Anita Fernandes. However, the new chairman did not deem it fit to elevate these three managers to the board for the time being.

He had been receiving mixed reviews about the integrity of Raj Dhingra, though he had no evidence to establish this. Raj had delivered everything and more to make the power division of their company one of the leading players in the country. As the former finance director, the chairman decided that he would personally spend more time observing Raj and tracking the various transactions that were being handled by him.

The chairman had also been hearing rumours about Sangeeta's personal life and though he was not really interested in it, he was worried to see the company's name in the gossip columns of a newspaper, where Sangeeta had been linked to a pilot. At the same time, she was delivering the bottom-line targets for her business and her division was adding very significantly to the valuation of Trust Corporation. He decided to observe her for a while before taking a call either way.

As far as HR was concerned, the chairman had always believed that this was a support function and while it must have a strong leader, he was not convinced that it should get a place on the board of directors.

Finally, to consolidate his own position on the board, the chairman broke with precedence and decided not to appoint a vice-chairman. He wanted to observe the board members and did not want to announce a successor so early. He decided that he would nominate the next chairman from his board of directors towards the end of his tenure.

There was also a more Machiavellian motive behind this move.

The chairman wanted to see how long he could continue as the head, and if he could beat the age of superannuation that had been established over the years. He had an excellent relationship with both international and Indian shareholders and given the outstanding performance of the company, he was confident that he would be able to get the board to go along with any recommendation he might decide to make for himself.

It was another matter that the chairman himself had known about his future ten years before he entered the corner office. He had had the benefit of being mentored by the previous chairman but he was not willing to give anyone else the same advantage.

~

Rahul

By 2007, Rahul and Lata had been married for twenty-five years.

They decided to host a large party for their friends and family to celebrate their silver wedding anniversary. They invited over 250 guests for their party and were pleasantly surprised to note that everyone accepted and made the extra effort to participate in their joy.

Although their marriage had been stormy in patches they had invested in their relationship, Lata far more than Rahul. They were perceived as a happy and content couple within the company as well as amongst their friends.

Their children, too, had made them proud. Both had completed their education and were employed in multinational companies. They were not dependent on their parents for anything.

~

Rahul's relationship with the chairman, as well as with the overseas shareholder of Trust Corporation, was excellent. He had allowed no controversies in his professional or personal life. Everyone expected Rahul to be anointed the vice-chairman of the company but the chairman had kept everyone guessing.

Every few months a rumour would be floated about

the possible entry of a top manager from another company because 'new blood would inject fresh thinking'. After every board meeting, another rumour would start that the American shareholder was sending an expatriate to take control of the company.

None of these rumours turned out to be true, but no announcement was forthcoming either.

Rahul continued to function as the director-in-charge of the alcohol division, bringing in record profits for the company year after year. There was not much innovation he could do in the business, but he took advantage of the tax laws of the country in consultation with Iqbal and launched several new products at various price points to address a much larger cross-section of the market.

~

As the new decade came to a close, there was concern in the parent company on Long Island, New York, about the leadership of their Indian subsidiary.

The chairman of the Indian company had served for almost a decade and was reaching the age of superannuation. He had not yet started the process of appointing a successor. This had led to several rounds of discussions and disagreements between the chairman and the overseas shareholder, though no action was taken by the parent company to precipitate matters.

Rahul and Iqbal were the only two directors on the board who could be eligible for consideration, unless the shareholders decided to bring in someone else.

At the request of the overseas shareholder, the company secretary called for an emergency meeting of the board to seek recommendations for the position of vice-chairman, but the chairman decided to defer taking a decision.

He was looking to extend his tenure further for a period of five years.

The American shareholder was not willing to go along with the chairman to give him an extension. Seeing the seriousness of the matter, the shareholder sent a senior director from the main board of the international group to meet with the Indian shareholders and impress upon them that changing the leadership of the Indian company was in everyone's best interests. Holding on to positions would affect succession planning throughout the organization and challenge the positive energy that existed in the management ranks.

After several parleys and discussions, the chairman agreed to step down on the agreed date when he realized that he would not be able to push his own case any longer.

The selected person would move directly to the position of chairman, without the benefit of serving as the vice-chairman under the mentorship of the chairman. He would have to learn the ropes directly on the job and at the same time, work to rebuild a complete board for the future. The shareholders also mandated that the company would never again be without a vice-chairman.

~

Raj

Raj was drinking more than ever.

He would drink when he was happy and he would drink when he was sad. He would drink when he was with people and he would drink when alone. He started to drink in the afternoons as well, before lunch. He had a whisky bottle hidden away in his bottom drawer at work. He would pour a little bit of alcohol into his morning coffee as well as his late afternoon coffee.

Alcohol consumed him completely, and it was almost as if his life was being sustained by the calories from his drinks. Though Trust Corporation was the largest alcohol manufacturer in India, the company did not permit consumption of alcohol in the office. It was also against excessive drinking.

Recognizing his drinking problem, Raj had sought help twice and without telling his company, he had started taking treatment. His liver had been affected by his addiction. Each time he abstained for a few months, but then returned to drinking with a vengeance.

Raj was also seeing Barbara more often. He had started asking her to meet him in other cities when he was travelling. He was still cautious about them travelling together, since the conversation he'd had with Anita about his relationship with Barbara still rankled in his mind. Though Barbara was no longer working for Trust Corporation, Raj decided that he must be extra careful in his relationship with her.

Barbara was also worried about Raj's drinking, though she was partly responsible for his slipping back every time. Her worry stemmed from the fact that she had not yet extracted her pound of flesh from him.

She knew he was making a lot of money and that the money was being sent to Lovely. She was troubled about the fact that none of this money was finding its way to her, barring a small amount for her upkeep. She also knew that she was the person Raj depended on and it was her shoulder that he would cry on when something was troubling him.

She had not yet used her trump card—telling him about their illegitimate son. The time had now come for her to play her cards sensibly. Sensing an opportunity when they were together in a hotel room in Mumbai, she took out a photograph of her son and showed it to him.

'Looks familiar?' she asked.

Raj looked at the photograph of a young boy in his late teens. He was shocked to see that the young man was a spitting image of himself.

'Who is he?' Raj asked apprehensively.

'Your son,' Barbara replied very calmly, watching his face turn ashen grey.

'What are you talking about?' he said hoarsely. 'This is completely untrue!' He could, however, see the striking resemblance with himself and knew that there was no point in denying this.

'You fathered him when we were working together in New Delhi, before you had me fired. You never gave me a chance to meet you after I was fired based on your false allegations of stealing your money,' Barbara responded.

'Why did you not tell me about this in the last ten years that we have been together again?' Raj wanted to know.

'If I had told you about him when we started meeting again, you would have stopped seeing me. While I have enjoyed being with you, I know that nothing in your life is permanent,' Barbara said.

'But I love you and care for you, Barbara. I want to meet my son,' he whispered.

Barbara laughed.

'You don't love anyone except yourself. You know that. As for meeting my son, you can forget about it. He will never know who his real father is,' she said. 'It is time for us to end our relationship, Raj. I expect you to transfer ₹2 crore to my account. I will avoid any further embarrassment for you in your company or with your wife by taking the secret of our son to my grave.'

Raj smiled to himself. What an amazing irony his life was.

He had spent a sum of ₹10 the first time he had paid for sex. He used to pay US$ 150 when he called a woman to his hotel room during his overseas travels.

Today, he was being asked to pay ₹2 crore for several sessions of sex with one woman, whom he had thought he cared for. He had assumed that she would be his mistress all his life, or for as long as he wanted.

The principle was the same. The rate had gone up significantly and his ability to pay had grown dramatically.

Raj was a coward.

Every time he was confronted with a problem, his first instinct was to run. He could not afford to have this information leaked to his wife or his company. He could deny his paternity in the short term but he knew that if a DNA test was carried out, conclusive proof would be made available. He decided that it would be more sensible to pay her off and close the chapter once and for all.

Barbara walked out of his life forever.

She'd had the last laugh.

~

Lovely was spending more than ever.

Raj was channelizing all the cash he was raking in from his underhand deals to her. He had worked out a system with his suppliers wherein they would directly deliver the money to his wife and she would send him a short message in code over the mobile phone.

Though Raj did not meet her as often as she would have liked to see him, her relationship with her husband had transitioned from one of not caring to one of grudging acceptance and sometimes admiration for her husband. She no longer blamed him for having left her and their children all alone over the past two decades. With unlimited money in her hand, she was willing to accept him in any avatar.

Her lavish lifestyle was beginning to get noticed by the elite of Chandigarh and questions were being asked on who she was and how she had suddenly emerged on the social scene. From a nondescript housewife like millions of others, she was suddenly the cynosure of all eyes because of her wealth.

She was buying property all over Punjab and every broker wanted to work with her. She was a buyer for agricultural land, apartments and commercial property. She was beginning to run out of names for registering properties, so she started using the names of her relatives and forging their signatures.

As Raj channelized more and more money to her, she started becoming rash with her investments.

The income tax authorities had been following all her purchases. They, too, wondered where she was getting so much money. There were rumours that her husband was sending a lot of his illegal wealth but there was no evidence to link him.

One morning Lovely saw six leather-jacketed men standing outside her gate.

'This is an income tax raid, madam,' said one of the officers, presenting his identity card and the warrant for the search.

They did not allow her to make any calls, nor was she permitted to move from the room she was sitting in, even to change her clothes. The raid lasted over eight hours and the officers found large sums of cash, gold, diamonds and property documents. All this was confiscated.

Lovely called Raj after the officers had gone and told him what had happened.

Raj panicked and said, 'Lovely, you cannot link any of this to me. I have a career and cannot let anything jeopardize it.

'If the income tax authorities call me, I will deny any involvement with you. In any case you and I have lived separate lives for almost thirty years,' he concluded.

Lovely knew her husband well.

She was surprised at herself that she had chosen to call him, expecting him to support her. She was a strong woman and knew she had the resources to fight her income tax battles. Besides, what the income tax officers had found was a small fraction of the wealth she had squirreled away in India and overseas.

She thought long and hard and decided that her life with Raj was over. She was a very wealthy woman. All the money that Raj had given her was hers alone. He had no access to it and she was certainly not going to let him anywhere near it.

She asked her lawyer to prepare the papers for their divorce.

When the documents came, she picked up her gold Mont Blanc fountain pen, signed them and broke the nib.

~

For nearly a decade, India had two power markets operating in parallel.

The inefficient public-sector utilities in the mainstream network were used by the politicians to dole out favours to the electorate, including free power for agriculture, thus bankrupting most of the government-owned power producers. In 2003, the Electricity Act made changes and allowed partial liberalization. The law permitted private power producers to sell power to private distributors and even directly to consumers. It also permitted private players to start trading in power.

This was a path-breaking piece of legislation.

Raj saw an opportunity for Trust Corporation once this law had been enacted. Trust was a large producer of power and could now start distribution, which would lead to significantly higher profits. The high-profile case of the now bankrupt Enron, at one stage one of the largest producers and distributors of power in the world, was staring them in the face, and he knew that he would have to counter this carefully when he went to the board of directors for a decision.

The board of directors had been reconstituted after the new chairman had taken over and unlike the previous six-member board, now there were only three. In addition to the chairman, the other two directors were Rahul Jain, director-in-charge of the alcohol division and Iqbal Mohammad, the finance director.

Raj had not been able to internalize that he would be pitching to his former batchmates.

He prepared a detailed presentation to the board of directors and said, 'Two decades of growth in the country has created a slew of middle-class households accustomed to air conditioning and television, and a host of industries that need to keep call centres or textile mills running. We should seriously consider setting up a distribution arm as a part of our power division.'

'How will we handle the huge thefts in the distribution business? We have so far been producers and we sell all the power to distributors and get our money. If we start distribution, how will we handle the losses?' asked Iqbal.

Iqbal had long suspected that Raj was making a lot of money in the power division. He was determined to stop Raj from going ahead with any new ventures which could give him more opportunities to line his pockets. He was also keen to ensure that Raj did not get an advantage to take a shot at the top job.

'We will have to set up systems and I have the political connections to make sure we find our way through the mess. If the political class allows us to do so, nobody will fret over the old state-run system going dark,' Raj concluded, hoping that his plan would be given speedy approval.

The board was not convinced, first about the project, and next about the ability of Raj to lead such a challenging initiative. They were concerned about Raj's alcoholism and all the issues surrounding his personal integrity.

Iqbal had carried out a very detailed and diligent investigation on Raj's financial transactions and while he had seen a trend in the increasing amounts of money being paid out, purportedly to the politicians, there was no way that he could establish this with any degree of certainty.

The chairman, in consultation with his colleagues on the board, decided to defer the decision to a later date.

Raj took this decision of the board as a personal affront. He was hurt more because his proposal had been blackballed by his own batchmates, his friends and colleagues for almost three decades.

He had also started to believe that he was indispensable to the company.

'There is no way that these people can run the complex power division without me,' he told himself. 'I am going to teach them a lesson and make them reverse their decision.'

Without thinking of the consequences, he decided to submit his resignation to the chairman.

Raj Malhotra's resignation was accepted immediately, with regret.

~

Raj sat and thought about the last thirty years of his life.

He wondered if he could look back at any part of his life with some degree of satisfaction. He had never been a good husband, a good father or a good son.

He had made a lot of money through illegal means but he had lost all of it to Lovely. She had taken away everything in the divorce. Since all the wealth was in cash and had no record, he could not lay his hands on anything. He was completely broke. Barring his final settlement from the company, he had nothing else to live on.

He had tried reaching out to his children, who were working and studying in Australia, but they had refused to have any contact with him. He had not been there when they needed him; now they wanted nothing to do with him.

He had fathered an illegitimate son with Barbara. In order to avoid any embarrassment he had succumbed to her blackmail and given her a large amount of cash. He had thought he loved Barbara but was shocked to hear from her that she had never forgotten how he had treated her when she'd worked for him as his secretary. All she had wanted in their second liaison was his money. She did not care for him, nor was she interested in any long-term relationship with him. He had been cruel to her and she had got her own back.

'What kind of a mother is she, not allowing the father of her child to meet his son?' he thought and yet, at the back of his mind, he understood her reasons.

His career had not worked out the way he had planned. He had started out with the aim of entering the corner office before he turned fifty. With his resignation from the company he had loved and worked for his entire life, this dream was over.

He went back to heavy drinking once again after spending several months in rehabilitation, and this time there was no one to check him or stop him from pouring 'one more drink', like Barbara used to.

Now, as he walked into his favourite bar and asked for a drink, he realized that all his friends, acquaintances and cronies who had hung around him and laughed at every joke he narrated had left him. When he tried to strike up a conversation with some of them sitting at the bar, they looked the other way.

No one wanted to be seen talking to him or associating with him.

He was a complete failure.

He walked to the bar and called for 100 ml each of whisky, rum and vodka. He mixed all three into one glass and gulped down the potent mixture in one shot. Then he rested his head on his hands and slumped on the bar counter.

The barman was the only friend he had left in the world.

Sangeeta

Sangeeta's personal life was a complete mess.

After separating from her husband, Major Ajay Sharma, she had decided that men were to be used for pleasure. She had been in and out of several relationships, some for the specific purpose of getting work done and others for sheer fun. She had no anchor in her life and no one to go home to every evening. Her parents, who had been pillars of strength for her, had passed away several years ago and she was now alone.

She had survived breast cancer. The surgery had removed all the affected areas and she had not let it affect her life. She had returned to the life of a normal young woman within a few months. Doctors had told Sangeeta that though the cancer in her breast had been removed, she must continue with regular annual check-ups.

'Breast cancer never really goes away. You have to be prepared that it may surface in the same place, or it may metastasize in another area. It may even lie dormant for a very long period of time,' they said.

When she had asked for more specific information, they were vague. 'We don't really know too much about cancer. We learn new things about this disease everyday.'

Sangeeta, though, did not go for her regular check-ups as

she was too busy with her work.

As she reached the age of forty-nine, she was asked by the HR department to go for a complete medical screening. While doing an endoscopy, doctors found a growth near her lungs, inside the wall of the intestine. They took a few samples and had these sent for a biopsy.

Sangeeta had a gut feeling that her cancer was back.

When the results arrived, her worst fears came true. The tumour was malignant and growing rapidly. The cancer this time was very aggressive and had metastasized into other parts of her body.

'Many women continue to live long, productive lives with metastasized breast cancer in this stage. It is also likely that your experience with treatment this time will be somewhat different from last time. There are so many options for your care and so many ways to chart your progress as you move through diagnosis, treatment and beyond,' her doctor explained.

'How long do I have, Doctor?' Sangeeta asked bluntly.

'No one can tell you how long you will live with metastatic disease. That's because every woman's experience is different. Some women live for more than a decade. Others for just a couple of years. But new and more effective treatments keep being developed. This means that you may do much better today than someone who had it only a few years ago,' her doctor continued.

Sangeeta took in this information without reacting. She understood the ramifications of what her doctor was telling her. She had to go home and process all this carefully and think about her life ahead. She knew that there was a finiteness that had come into her life. While she knew that everyone had a limited lifespan, hers was shorter than others.

Her life had now been defined within a time frame.

The company offered to pay for all the expenses for her treatment anywhere in the world. Sangeeta chose to stay back in Delhi, so that she could continue with her treatment and not let her work suffer.

~

The software division of the company had done well when compared to what had been expected by the chairman and the shareholders of the company. However, when its performance was compared to the software majors of the country, it dwarfed into insignificance.

While the major software companies were delivering billions of dollars in profit, Sangeeta was delivering profits in the low hundreds of millions of dollars. She was never able to take advantage of the valuation that other software majors had been given by the markets because her business group was a part of a conglomerate, and valuations of the alcohol and power business were far lower than the software business.

While her performance within the company was generally applauded, financial analysts had started to give their opinion regularly and always compared her business to the software majors of the country.

'The software business of Trust Corporation is a laggard in the country. It is not giving the right valuations that the shareholders of the company deserve,' one analyst wrote.

'The company should seriously consider spinning off its software business into a separate unit to unlock its true potential,' wrote another analyst.

Iqbal, in his capacity as the finance director, was charged with the responsibility of answering these queries. He had always been wary of Sangeeta and jealous of her rapid rise. He had never learned to appreciate the success of any woman and Sangeeta's success rankled him, even though she was from his batch.

Iqbal believed that a woman's place was in the house. He had not changed his thinking since the time he had been married and working with aggressive, successful and beautiful colleagues unnerved him, making him very self-conscious.

He decided to kill two birds with one stone.

He recommended to the chairman that the software business should be spun off into a separate company as a wholly owned subsidiary. He further recommended that Sangeeta be appointed the new managing director of the subsidiary company.

'We will be able to address the concerns of the analysts. This will create significant value for the company and our share price will shoot up. At an appropriate time, the company could consider issuing shares to the public in its software subsidiary,' he continued.

'A public issue of shares will also release a lot of cash for our organization,' he told the overseas shareholder and the chairman.

I will also be able to get Sangeeta out of my way once she moves to the subsidiary, he thought.

The chairman liked both his recommendations and after consulting the international shareholder, he decided to go ahead with the restructuring of the company.

Sangeeta knew that she had been sidetracked from her career. She got to know that Iqbal had been the architect of this grand plan. She grudgingly accepted that the proposal was in the best interest of the company, though her career had been sacrificed in the process.

She was being offered the position of managing director of the newly created Trust Software Corporation, but she knew that her dream of joining the board of Trust Corporation and eventually becoming its first woman chairperson was over.

Though her cancer had recurred and she would need to spend a lot of time on her treatment, which would lead to slowing down on her work commitments, she blamed Iqbal for the final nail in the coffin of her once promising and illustrious career.

~

Sangeeta poured herself a stiff Lagavulin malt whisky as she sat at home after her meeting with the chairman. She had always liked the strong peaty aroma of this whisky and preferred it neat in a heavy cut-glass whisky tumbler.

'This is an incredible opportunity for you, Sangeeta. You will be the first woman to head a large software company in India,' the chairman had told her when offering her the position of managing director.

'I need you in the company to build our business. You know every customer personally and you can lead this transition well from a division to a wholly owned subsidiary. I also trust you to carry all our value systems into the new company,' he had continued.

'Give me one day to think about this, please,' Sangeeta had requested.

The chairman was surprised at her reaction. He could not imagine anyone else fitting the job better but he agreed to meet her again the following morning.

Sangeeta finished her first drink in one shot. She could feel the warm glow of the whisky flowing down her throat and into her stomach. She had been advised by her doctor not to drink because of her cancer, but as she had never conformed to anything she had been asked to do, her doctor's advice was no different.

She poured herself another drink, this one larger than the first.

As she thought about her life, her first thoughts went to Major Ajay Sharma, her former husband. She had been very unfair to him. She recognized that he had made every effort to save their marriage and she had done virtually nothing.

Neither of them had stayed in touch after their bitter divorce.

She had kept track of Ajay's career in the army though, and over the last few years he had featured prominently in the newspapers. He was seen as a hero in recent skirmishes across the border and had been applauded for the work he had done to quell riots in another part of the country. She had cut out and saved a recent news article, which talked about her former husband being in contention for the chief of army staff.

'I wanted the chairman's room so badly and you never wanted the chief's position,' she thought, looking at his photograph. 'Now it looks like you will make it to the corner office in army headquarters. I know that I have definitely not made it.'

She wondered how her life would have shaped out if she had been beside Ajay and had supported him in his rise to the top. She had no regrets in pursuing her own dream at the cost of their relationship, and this surprised her even as she looked back.

She thought of her parents, and the wonderful and pampered childhood she'd had. She missed her father's warm comforting hug and her mother's wise words. She had always dismissed anything her mother told her and now she regretted not listening to her.

She thought of all the men in her life, including the guy from IIT who had raped her, but was surprised to find that none of them were more than a blur.

She thought of her pilot friend Arun with a little more fondness because of his being a recent memory, but she could not recall much about him either.

She thought of her cancer.

She had fought it and won the first time. Though she always knew that no one ever triumphs over cancer permanently, she had hoped that she would be the first person to beat the odds. She was not unduly shocked when the doctor had told her that the cancer was back, this time with a vengeance.

'You will have to restart chemotherapy and radiation, the sooner the better,' her doctor had said.

But she did not have the determination or the will to fight cancer again.

She looked at her whisky glass, which was almost empty. She got up to fill her glass a third time. Then she walked to her Bose music system plugged to her iPhone and switched on soulful Hemant Kumar melodies, her favourite music.

She picked up her revolver, which she had purchased so easily at an arms shop in USA. The salesman had told her that the Smith & Wesson 'AirLite' was the best revolver for women. It had a very light trigger. She opened the chamber of the revolver and put in a single bullet. She put the muzzle of the revolver into her mouth. She closed her eyes and said a silent prayer, thinking of Ajay and her parents.

Then she gently squeezed the trigger.

Iqbal

Iqbal had not bothered about his weight despite his health scare and continued to eat heavy, oily food. His asthma had increased significantly and he constantly carried a cortisone inhaler with him. His blood pressure always remained high. His diabetes was out of control, since he refused to exercise or regulate his diet. He was on regular insulin injections before every meal. His toes and the webbing between them had cuts, which were not healing on account of his diabetes.

He did not seem to care at all for his health.

Life for Samina remained unchanged even after her husband was promoted to the top job in the finance department.

She had never been encouraged by Iqbal to get to know any of his colleagues or their wives. After so many years, she had lost interest as well. She found it strange when she received so many calls from the wives of Iqbal's subordinates to congratulate her on her husband's promotion.

'Thank you very much for your wishes, but why are you calling me? I have not played any role in my husband's career,' she told every surprised caller.

Over the last two decades, Iqbal had successfully alienated himself completely from his family.

He did not remember when he had last celebrated their

wedding anniversary or sent Samina flowers on her birthday. He had no recollection of the birthdays of his three sons. He was barely aware of where they had studied and he had no idea of their grades or what they wanted to do. He knew that all his sons had completed their education and had started working, but he did not care to find out what they were doing.

He had never felt the need to play the role of a dutiful parent. That was Samina's job and he could not change his thinking at this late stage in life.

As Iqbal turned fifty, his eldest son turned twenty-five. His younger sons were twenty-four and twenty-three.

The boys had built a separate life for themselves. They had purchased a separate apartment in the same city without telling their father. They, along with their mother, spent several weeks together in the new apartment, setting it up. They moved all their important belongings to their new home, once again without his knowledge.

The three started spending some nights in their apartment and Iqbal was so busy at work that he never noticed their absence from his home.

All the boys were fiercely protective about their mother and had a lot of pent-up anger for the ill-treatment they had seen her receive from their father all their lives. Iqbal had never spoken properly to their mother as long as they could remember and they had seen him slap her quite often. They would all go and sit around her in the dark corner of a room, as sobs racked her body, and they were never able to understand why she had to take so much insult from their father.

One evening, Iqbal came home very angry after losing money in the stock markets and as always, he started to vent his anger on Samina. When his youngest son decided to intervene,

Iqbal slapped him across his face, without a second thought.

That was the last straw for Samina and her sons. They walked out of Iqbal's house, never to return again.

~

Iqbal had made it to the board ahead of three of his batchmates, Sangeeta, Raj and Anita, though one year after Rahul. He was convinced that he was the right person to occupy the corner office after his mentor, the current chairman.

He recognized that his only competition was Rahul, who was running the company's largest and most profitable business. Rahul could rightfully stake his claim and he, Iqbal, had to figure out a way to stop his batchmate, who had never shown the slightest chink in his armour over the last two and a half decades.

Based on a rumour that he had heard about Rahul's heart condition, Iqbal had sent a trusted assistant to Singapore and ferreted out copies of the bills of Rahul's heart surgery. He had Rahul's accounts checked very carefully and was surprised to find no claim for these medical expenses.

Hiding a medical condition was considered a serious lapse in the company, more so if done by a member of top management. Iqbal made a mental note to use this valuable information sometime in the future.

He had played a role in uncovering the financial issues linked to Raj and though it had never been established, he had successfully sown the seeds of doubt about Raj's integrity in the minds of the chairman and the board.

Then there was the other matter of Raj's wife Lovely, who had suddenly come into a lot of money. The general communication from Raj was that she had received a huge inheritance from a distant relative. Iqbal had investigated her entire family and not found any evidence of wealth. He came to know about the income-tax raids on Raj's wife and managed to get a copy of the panchnama through his sources. He sent this anonymously to the chairman.

He had never seen Anita as a threat professionally. She was weak and uncertain of herself. The shareholders would never even consider her for the top job. He also knew that she had a weak spot for her good-for-nothing husband. Iqbal had copies of Michael's personal invoices at the club, which had been charged to the company. If the need ever arose, Iqbal had enough to attack Anita via her husband.

Sangeeta was another matter altogether. Iqbal was worried about her. Though she had not made it to the board of directors, he was sure it was only a matter of time before Sangeeta was promoted. She had come back as the proverbial dark horse several times and surprised everyone. Her business was also performing very well.

~

As the finance director, Iqbal had complete control of the treasury function. The company had large cash surpluses and these were invested in various financial instruments to earn higher yields and augment the bottom line.

'We have to make our money work for us,' Iqbal would tell his teams.

The broker community in the country was always trying to get close to him. One favour from Iqbal could start channelizing the surplus funds of the company through the broker's firm, resulting in large brokerage fees.

One smart broker who had been introduced to Iqbal

sometime back at a party decided to try something different and more direct. He walked up to him with an envelope in his hand.

'Sir, I was checking the prices of Infrastructure Builders Company Limited based on an insider tip. I tried to call you but was not able to get through to you. I decided to buy 50,000 shares in your name. The share price went up by ₹10 within an hour of my purchasing them. I sold these shares immediately and you have made a profit of ₹5,00,000. Here, I have brought the cheque for you,' he said.

Iqbal was shrewd enough to recognize what the broker was saying. He knew that the broker wanted to do other business with the company and was offering him a bribe in a covert manner. Instead of rebuking the broker, he said, 'Thank you very much. That is what good friends are for. I have also been following the performance of the same company but have not had the time to call you to make an investment.' He took the envelope and put it into his coat pocket.

The broker knew that he had managed to get the break he was looking for.

Iqbal had found a trusted individual to play the stock markets without drawing any attention to himself.

Over the next few years, Iqbal and the broker put together a series of deals for the company. Some of these deals were done quietly in Iqbal's name. If a personal deal went sour, the losses would be booked in the name of the company and if a company deal made huge profits, a small part of the profits would be booked in Iqbal's name.

It was a foolproof mechanism and Iqbal started to put away a tidy sum of money. He opened a separate bank account and instructed the broker to deposit his ill-gotten gains into the account. As his greed got the better of him, he started moving significantly larger sums of money from the company's earnings to his own.

No one could find out about such transactions and the broker, in his own interest, would keep his mouth shut.

When the international markets crashed, Iqbal thought it was time to unwind his own positions and called the broker to stop all further deals.

'Please close all my accounts with you,' he told the broker.

'That would not be possible, sir,' said the broker. 'You have open positions worth several crore rupees and in order to unwind these, you will have to pay a lot of cash. If you instruct, I can recover this money from the company.'

Iqbal was shocked at the size of his exposure in the markets. He had not realized that his open positions had become so large. He did not have the money to square up his accounts. The amounts were too large to debit to the company too.

He screamed at the broker, losing his volatile temper once again, 'How could you allow this to happen? I am stopping all further business with you. Also I will blacklist you in my company, and we will not work with you either.'

He slammed the phone down and refused to take any further calls.

The broker, a shrewd businessman, had planned for such a contingency. In order to protect himself, he had kept copies of every transaction note on Iqbal's personal account locked away in his safe. He had also kept copies of the handwritten instructions from Iqbal for any trades and adjustments in the accounts.

Unable to handle the personal affront and the loss of his business, the broker made photocopies of every transaction document and bank deposit slip. He put all these incriminating documents in an envelope and mailed them to the chairman.

The broker had lost everything because Iqbal refused to honour his financial commitments. He was labelled a defaulter by the regulatory bodies. Financial markets are never kind to defaulters. He was clear that since he had been destroyed, he would ensure that Iqbal would not survive either.

The letter from the broker reached the chairman with all its startling disclosures. When Iqbal was called to the chairman's office for an explanation, he tried to discredit the broker and deny all allegations. The chairman, who had been a finance professional as well as Iqbal's mentor, realized that the papers in front of him were potentially explosive and could destroy his own career, as well the credibility of the company.

Insider trading was a serious offence in the country and the chairman knew that stock exchange officials would immediately get involved in this investigation. He had to take every possible step to protect Trust Corporation at all costs.

The chairman came to an immediate decision.

'Iqbal, I have no option but to suspend you from the services of the company with immediate effect. This looks like a clear case of fraud,' he said. 'I have already informed the group finance director in Long Island, New York, and he concurs with my decision.

'I wish you had not let me down so badly. How could you possibly do something so stupid and hope to get away with it? I trusted you completely and had great plans for you,' he added as an afterthought. 'You need to be completely absolved from these allegations before I can let you come back into the company.'

Iqbal bowed his head and said nothing.

He knew that his career was over.

~

Iqbal Mohammad lay on the hospital bed, deep in thought, looking back at his life.

He had suffered an acute asthma attack within minutes of being suspended from his job. News of his suspension had spread like wildfire through the company. Such a move was unprecedented but then, so was his crime. Never in the history of the company had a finance manager, leave alone a finance director, been charged with insider trading and fraud.

Iqbal had called several political leaders for help. He had tried to use his minority status to protect himself, hoping that someone would raise the issue as an 'unfair reprisal of the minority community'.

No leader was willing to come and stand up for him in such a clear matter of fraud. He was too hot a potato and had to be dropped immediately.

He thought of his parents and brothers. Because of his intense anger against his brothers, he had refused to keep in touch with them or their families. He thought about the loss of his family wealth and his physical abuse at school and wondered why he had not been able to put these behind him and keep in touch with his family. He could have been a different person had he removed all the negativity that he carried within him.

He thought of Samina and his sons. He had never cared for his family and had taken his wife and sons for granted all their lives. He regretted slapping his youngest son, which had led Samina and his three children to walk out of his life forever. He regretted not having invested any time in the lives of his sons.

However, he still did not feel any regret for treating his wife badly. He had been brought up to think that women must serve their men and he believed that he had been a good provider for his wife.

His wife and his sons wanted nothing to do with him. He had tortured and terrorized them enough all through their lives, and now they did not even come to see him in the hospital.

As long as he was rising within the company, he had not needed anyone, family or friends. He was content by himself. His cronies at work kept him entertained all the time and made sure they said what he wanted to hear. Now that he was all alone and wanted someone to talk to, no one was there to spend any time with him. No one had come to visit him in the hospital.

He had lost everything, but he had to prepare for a long battle ahead to clear his name, which he knew was impossible.

He knew that he was very unwell.

His doctor had warned him to take care of his health a few years back, but he had ignored the advice. His obesity, combined with his high sugar level, asthma and high blood pressure, was a killer.

He was alone in the world and without his family he had lost the will to live.

He closed his eyes in submission.

~

Anita

Michael was finding it very difficult to reconcile himself to life after a stroke. With loving care from Anita and regular physiotherapy, as well as speech and language therapy, he had been able to regain most of the functions of his body. However, he was constantly tired and sad.

Barring a slight twitch of his left lower lip and a barely perceptible tremor in his right hand, he looked normal. He had lost a little weight, and Anita found him to be even more handsome than he had been when they got married.

However, mentally Michael was a complete wreck.

'How could I have been affected by a stroke? I was such a fit man,' he would keep telling himself and his wife.

'But you are absolutely fine,' she would reply, trying to get him to break out of his self-pity.

'What do you know?' he would shout angrily.

'I was such a fit person all my life, and now I am completely dependent on you,' Michael would say, without thinking for one moment that financially, he had in fact, always been completely dependent on Anita. She had provided for his every need, including his clothes and spending money, from the day they had got married.

No amount of counselling from his wife would help Michael

accept that he was getting better and that he should return to a normal life as soon as possible.

Michael's strong bond with their daughter was also getting frayed.

While Anita was willing to put up with his anger and frustration, their sixteen-year-old daughter, though accepting some of her father's mood swings, was not willing to take his negativity any longer. She was studying in a residential school and chose to stay back most weekends instead of coming home to be with her parents.

Less than six months later, Michael had another stroke, which left the left side of his body completely paralysed. He was rushed to hospital in a critical condition and the doctors were not sure he would be able to survive. He managed to pull through, but this time when he returned home, he was unable to do anything for himself. He needed help for everything, including sitting up in bed. His speech was slurred and every word was long-drawn-out, making comprehension near impossible. Only Anita was able to interpret what he wanted and she was not around all the time.

This time it was Anita's turn to question God.

'I have always been a strong believer in you, Lord. Why are you testing me so much and when will you ever finish?' she would ask Him every morning when she woke up.

Always a strong believer in God, she renewed her prayers to Him with unmatched passion. She would go to church every morning on her way to work and back. She would light a candle and pray for Michael's speedy recovery. She never missed the morning and evening service every Sunday and she made it a point to go for confession as well. She would tell the priest everything, as she sought absolution from even the most mundane transgression.

After his first stroke, Michael had been through mood swings and would often see himself as a liability on the family. Anita had had to manage him, as well her own moods and those of her daughter.

His second stroke had been much more severe and it was as if he no longer had the will to fight. He lost partial control of his bladder too and it was up to Anita or the nurse she had hired to wash and change him several times a day.

Michael had become an invalid and was incapable of taking care of himself any longer.

Given Anita's commitment to work and her long hours in the office as the head of the human resources function, she agonized about how to handle her husband's daily health needs. While she could continue with a full-time nurse, there was a chance Michael might suffer yet another stroke. Besides, the financial burden of his ill-health was beginning to strain her already limited financial resources. The company had a good medical scheme, but it was not intended for unlimited care for a manager or the family.

One of the doctors recommended that Anita consider moving Michael to a home for physically-challenged people, where he would be able to live with patients like himself and get good care from a group of dedicated nurses and doctors. She found it difficult to accept moving her husband of over twenty-five years to a home. However, she did go and visit one such place and was impressed to see the care being offered to the patients.

After an instance of negligence by the nurse, which led to Michael falling off his bed and cutting his forehead when Anita was not at home, she came to a conclusion. She decided that she would move Michael to the home.

'Michael, my darling, looks like the time has come for us to part ways,' she said. 'I hope you will be able to forgive me for moving you to a home, but I also hope you will understand that I have tried very hard and find it impossible to care for you the way I would like to, given my commitments at work. Our finances are also very strained, Michael, after meeting all your expenses. I cannot give up my work to look after you, since we have no reserves.'

Michael could see, hear and understand everything that was going on but could not say anything, since he had completely lost the power of speech. Anita saw a tear roll down his cheek.

The expression in his eyes went from sadness to anger and finally to resignation.

Anita accompanied him to the home for the physically challenged and after getting Michael admitted, she went to his room to settle him in.

She signed all the papers and paid for one year in advance. She would continue to pay for his stay at the home all his life.

It was as if he had gone out of her life forever.

~

Anita Fernandes had seen a meteoric rise in the HR function and was the first woman to have broken the glass ceiling in her function in the country.

The Government of India had recognized Anita's contribution to the field of human resources and she was called regularly to consult on matters of national importance by the ministry of human resources.

As the new boss of the HR function, Anita was keen to leave her mark. She had not been promoted to the board like Rahul and Iqbal and she thought she had being discriminated against since she was a woman. About Sangeeta not being promoted as well, she rationalized that Sangeeta's performance was possibly not up to the mark.

Anita had been trained to think of employees first, before any other consideration. Her boss, the new chairman, was a finance person by training and conditioned into thinking of cost first. The chairman had never got along with her ex-boss and mentor, the former director of human resources, who had resigned when the chairman had taken over the reins of the company.

The new chairman had always felt that Trust Corporation was being over-generous to its employees and wanted Anita to start rationalizing the numbers and cost structures of the company in line with contemporary thinking in India. He also wanted to start looking again at the significant perquisites that the company offered its management.

Anita was forced, much against her wishes, into working on a proposal to remove perquisites like furnished accommodation, club memberships, reporting trips and family vacations for staff located at alcohol-manufacturing facilities and power-generation facilities in rural India.

The chairman then asked her to move every employee to a flat 'cost to company' package and bring in the concept of a variable pay to reward the better performers. She was taken aback when she saw support for this proposal from the other two board members, Rahul and Iqbal.

The last straw, from her perspective, was when she was asked to stop offering the attractive company pension scheme to all future employees.

She rebelled.

'We have already taken away all the perquisites from our

staff members and put pressure on them to accept a variable component in the salary. Now you want me to stop pensions for new recruits?' she argued.

'This is not the company I had joined in 1980. You cannot change its basic fibre. Without a strong retirement programme, how can you expect any manager to spend his entire life here? How will we get future leaders?' she continued.

The chairman and the board members were not willing to listen to her.

'The country has changed, Anita. Young people are not looking for lifetime employment with a single company any longer, and you should know it. We need HR policies to retain our people, but for that we need to engage them. You know that we are not the highest paymasters, so you need to think out of the box. Paying higher salaries is never the answer to good HR practices,' said Rahul.

'As the HR manager, you have to look at the costs we have to bear for our people, Anita. Remember that while you are accountable to the employees, as top management, we have much greater accountability to our shareholders who have invested in the company,' said Iqbal.

Anita looked at the chairman, her eyes pleading with him to overrule his other two colleagues.

'Get real, Anita. This is 2010, not 1980. Look at the significant changes taking place in our country. You have to learn to change and not continue to live in prehistoric times like your old boss used to,' he said. He had never been fond of his weak head of human resources and was always putting her under a lot of pressure.

'I must have your fresh manpower numbers and manpower cost proposals within a week,' he ordered.

Anita left the boardroom in quiet contemplation, thinking of what she should be doing. After this interaction with the three directors, including the chairman, she knew that her elevation to the board of directors of the company was never going to happen. Her position was far too divergent from the board and they knew that she was unlikely to change her stance, given the old-school thinking she had been brought up in.

She knew she could not fight the board. She also knew that she would not be able to compromise on her values and the way she wanted to mentor people.

She had two choices.

The first was to bend and accept what was required of her, and follow the chairman's instructions each time she was asked to change or destroy one more people-friendly policy of the company.

Her second choice was to stick to her convictions and resign from the services of the company she loved.

She decided on the second option and sent in her resignation to the chairman.

Her resignation was accepted.

~

Anita stood all by herself in her company apartment, looking around. She knew that she would have to vacate it soon after her resignation. She had not planned for her retirement. She had not purchased a house, so she would have to look for rented accommodation.

She was not even sure where she wanted to settle down for the rest of her life. Her first thought was to be near Michael, but she pushed it away. She wanted to be free for the first time in her life.

She sat down and looked back at her life over the last thirty years.

She'd had a wonderfully happy childhood and entered Trust Corporation with a lot of hope and expectation.

On the professional front, while she had not made it to the corner office or even to the board of directors, she had risen to the top of her function and was considered an authority in her field in the country, which was no mean achievement.

She regretted that she had not been able to carry through her conviction of protecting the old HR structures and value systems for the employees of the company as her predecessors had done. Future generations of HR managers would castigate her for her failures and for letting her function down.

Anita was getting old and her knees were beginning to trouble her. Her small frame had always been vulnerable to minor ailments, but arthritis was new and the pain in her knees and joints was sometimes debilitating. She had also been asthmatic, but other than keeping an inhaler with her at all times, she had not bothered much about it.

She had never had any time to think about herself and she had never cared to make friends, either within the company or outside. Her social life was a complete zero and she had no one to turn to for advice or counsel. She had lived a large part of her personal life looking after the excessive needs of her selfish husband. Sometimes she wondered how life would have turned out for her if she had not married Michael. Had she been right in agreeing to support him financially? Had she made him into a good-for-nothing man who had become so totally dependent on her that he stopped even making an effort to be gainfully employed?

Anita's daughter was now twenty-one years old and in

college. She had left the upbringing of her daughter to her husband. She had been far too busy at her work, chasing her dreams, and she was grateful that he had taken the responsibility of bringing up their child.

After she left her paralysed husband in a home, she had tried to reach out to her daughter. Both of them had found nothing in common. Anita realized that she had been never around for her daughter, barring a short period when Michael had been unwell. She had not realized that over the years, she would get so totally alienated from her child. She had prided herself on being an excellent HR manager, but seemed to have gone horribly wrong when it came to managing the relationship with her own daughter.

Her daughter had built a life of her own with a group of friends and blocked her mother out of her life. She also blamed Anita for abandoning Michael. She was not willing to give her mother a second chance.

~

Anita decided to seek solace in her church.

She approached the Mother Superior of her local convent to explore the possibility of joining the service of God as a nun, but was advised that the convent would not be able take anyone who was over forty years of age and married.

'There are many other ways to serve God, and you could come and work in the church every day,' she was advised.

Yet another door was closed for her.

What will I do? Where will I live? she thought.

Is all this retribution for not looking after my husband? Did I make a mistake in sending him to a home for the physically challenged? she wondered.

She thought of Mother Teresa's lines, which she had noted down in her small diary:

- *People are often unreasonable, illogical and self-centred; forgive them anyway.*
- *If you are kind, people may accuse you of selfish, ulterior motives; be kind anyway.*
- *If you are successful, you will win some false friends, and some true enemies; succeed anyway.*
- *What you spend years building, someone could destroy overnight; build anyway.*
- *If you find serenity and happiness, they may be jealous; be happy anyway.*
- *The good you do today, people will often forget tomorrow; do good anyway.*
- *Give the world the best you have, and it may never be enough; give the best anyway.*
- *You see, in the final analysis, it is between you and God; it is never between you and them anyway.*

She decided to give up all her worldly possessions and dedicate her life to God. She prayed that He would never abandon her.

~

Epilogue

Rahul woke up with a start a few minutes before 6 a.m. without waiting for his alarm clock to go off. He switched it off instead. He lay in bed, looking up at the ceiling.

Today was his day.

Late last evening, he had been informed that the shareholders of the company, led by the international and majority shareholder, had unanimously appointed him as chairman of the board of Trust Corporation, a multi-business, multi-billion-dollar conglomerate with business interests in India and several other neighbouring countries.

As a young starry-eyed management trainee who had joined the company thirty years ago, it had been his dream to reach the pinnacle of the company and drive its successful businesses, leaving his imprint on the indelible corporate and business landscape painted by so many of his illustrious predecessors. He had dreamt of sitting in the corner office, and this office was now his.

He turned and looked at Lata, his wife of thirty years, sleeping next to him, a look of calmness on her face. She had been his partner all his working life. He knew that while she would support him completely as he took charge as the chairman, she would have been equally happy if he was not in that position.

'Thank you, Lata,' he whispered to her.

He had been a very selfish husband, though unlike a lot of his friends whose marriages had fallen apart through the corporate journey, his marriage with Lata had stayed solid and secure. Their children had turned out well; both of them were settling into their respective careers. He gave all the credit for holding his marriage and family together to his wife. Left to him, he would have destroyed their relationship and family in the pursuit of his career.

He had sacrificed everything for his career and it was his wife who had held him, their fragile marriage, their children and their home together.

Yet, as he looked back at the last thirty years, staring at the ceiling and thinking of how he would plan his first day and his triumphant entry into the hallowed corridors of the corporate office, thoughts of all his colleagues he had shared good and bad times with flashed before his eyes. How many people and careers had he trampled over and how many games had he played? He thought of all the skeletons in his cupboard. He had wronged so many people in his life.

He could not remember when he had stepped into the public domain, where he had lost all his sense of privacy. He was always surrounded by colleagues, press and people employed in other companies whenever he travelled. Yet he could not think of a single friend whom he could rely upon or call to discuss anything personal.

Had it all been worth it?

Suddenly, fatigue crept over him and he closed his eyes, forcing himself to think of the day ahead and trying to wish away all the nagging thoughts of guilt and negativity. He had dreamt of becoming the chairman of this company from the very first day that he had joined as a management trainee and now he had achieved his dream.

Not many people could say this. This was what he had worked for all his life.

He had won.

The board of directors and the shareholders, in one unanimous voice, had selected him to lead the complex business group. He knew that he was the best to lead the company and provide it a new direction. He knew that thousands of employees in the many locations around the country would look up to him for leadership and follow his instructions and directions. He was comfortable with his relationships at the political and bureaucratic levels and knew that he had their support. He was acknowledged by his peers in the Indian industry and overseas. He and his wife were socially well-accepted.

Yet, why did he have so many doubts?

He thought of his four batchmates—Raj Dhingra, Sangeeta Malhotra, Iqbal Mohammad and Anita Fernandes. They had joined the company together and worked together for over three decades. They had shared good times and bad times. They had travelled together in India and overseas. They had shared confidences and revelled in one another's achievements.

After working together for about a decade, somewhere, their camaraderie had changed to competitiveness, which he had rationalized to himself as normal. All four of them had fallen by the wayside in their journey.

He thought of what had happened to them.

Raj Dhingra had always loved life in the fast lane and, as was his penchant, had turned to alcohol. Raj had faced several corruption scandals, though no one in the company had ever been able to prove anything. Raj's wife was under income tax investigation for wealth significantly beyond her known sources of income and Rahul had no illusions about where the money had come from. Raj had resigned from the company to go into rehabilitation but was not able to stay off alcohol. He could be seen sitting alone in a bar every evening.

Sangeeta Malhotra, the beautiful, lonely and intense Sangeeta, had not been able to handle her failure at making it to the top job, though she had been offered the CEO position of their software subsidiary. She had also not taken the recurrence of her cancer very well and had committed suicide, shooting herself through the back of her head from her mouth, in her company apartment.

Iqbal Mohammad, the brilliant yet warped financial genius, had been admitted into a hospital for care for his multiple ailments. It was unlikely that he would get well soon or come out of the hospital, ready to rejoin work. Even if he did recover from his illness, he would spend the rest of his life fighting legal battles for his financial scandal. He had lost his loyal wife Samina and his wonderful sons. After years of physical and mental abuse, she had taken their children and walked out on him, leaving him alone in the hospital.

Anita Fernandes had seen a meteoric rise in human resources and was the first woman to have broken the glass ceiling in her function. Though she had not made it to the board of directors of the company, she had reached the apex of her function. But had refused to move with the times in her career and had paid the price. After a rocky marriage, she had finally admitted her husband into a home for the physically challenged. She had given up everything, turned to Christ and surrendered her life to Him.

Rahul felt very lonely as he thought of the five young people who had started out together. Only he was left standing at the top of the victory stand with none of his batchmates by his side.

Why had all of them lost the race? What had he done right?

Why had they not been able to handle their failure? Would he have been able to handle his failure differently if he had not won?

Was the top corporate job the only defining moment of success in an otherwise boring and routine professional life?

There was a feeling of hollowness in his victory.

Had he really won at the cost of all his friends? Was he the best person to run the company, a job that all five of them had aspired for? Thirty years after he had run the gauntlet and come out the winner, he wondered whether the price he had paid had been worth what he had aspired for and achieved.

Had this race made up for all the sacrifices he had made of his family, his friends, his colleagues and his personal time? He had seen a shakeout when both his predecessors had taken over as the chairman and he guessed that this was to be expected.

He knew that there were no answers to all these questions.

He closed his eyes for a few minutes of quiet thought, prayer, contemplation, meditation and introspection. In accordance with his habit, he recited the Hanuman Chalisa, counting each of the forty verses on his fingertips.

Jai Hanuman Gyan Gun Sagar
Jai Kapis Tihu Lok Ujagar
Ram Doot Atulit Bal Dhama
Anjani Putra Pavan Sut Nama

His immediate and first task would be to have trusted people search the rooms of all the former board members to find and destroy any incriminating evidence that they might have left.

He was particularly keen to search Iqbal's office.

His second task as he walked into the corner office would be to appoint five new members to the board of directors to fill all the vacant positions, and elevate one of these five to the position of vice-chairman.

People would come and people would go, but Trust Corporation would exist, thrive and go on forever.

He was aware that the phone next to his bedside would start to ring soon.

A new, yet final, phase of his professional life was just beginning.

www.ingramcontent.com/pod-product-compliance
Lightning Source LLC
LaVergne TN
LVHW090938080826
845145LV00003B/793

* 9 7 8 8 1 2 9 1 2 4 7 7 7 *